ONE WAY TO GET YOUR ATTENTION . . .

Knowing "Reverend" Huckfield to be a member of the gang and—and according to information supplied by Belle—not the least dangerous of them, the Kid was not taken unawares. Thumbing back the hammer again while turning the short barrel of the Webley, he directed the second .450 bullet into the center of the gaunt man's forehead. Without speaking, as Huckfield was spinning lifeless to the floor, he swung the smoking weapon to encompass and cause the remaining pair of "guests" to freeze into immobility.

"Stand still, all of you!" Belle commanded in echo to the second shot, still retaining the 'Spanish' accent as an integral part of her scheme. She thrust her hand into the open mouth of her reticule. Bringing it out grasping a small bottle filled with a thick, dark brown liquid, she pushed off the glass stopper with her thumb and went on. "This contains the only antidote for *curare* there is to be found *anywhere* in Kansas. Unless you do as I say, I will pour it on the floor and the 'Duke' will die in agony!"

List of J.T. Edson titles in chronological and categorical sequence:

ARIZONA RANGE WAR
ARIZONA GUN LAW
( )

Waco series

WACO'S BADGE
SAGEBRUSH SLEUTH
ARIZONA RANGER
WACO RIDES IN
( )
THE DRIFTER
DOC LEROY, M.D.
HOUND DOG MAN

Calamity Jane series

TEXAS TRIO
COLD DECK, HOT LEAD
THE BULL WHIP BREED
TROUBLE TRAIL
THE COW THIEVES
THE HIDE AND HORN SALOON
CUT ONE, THEY ALL BLEED
CALAMITY SPELLS TROUBLE
WHITE STALLION, RED MARE
THE REMITTANCE KID
THE WHIP AND THE WAR LANCE
THE BIG HUNT

Waxahachie Smith series

NO FINGER ON THE TRIGGER
SLIP GUN
( )
CURE THE TEXAS FEVER

Alvin Dustine "Cap" Fog series

ALVIN FOG, TEXAS RANGER
RAPIDO CLINT
THE JUSTICE OF COMPANY "Z"
( )

CAP FOG, TEXAS RANGER, MEET
  MR. J.G. REEDER
THE RETURN OF RAPIDO CLINT
  AND MR. J.G. REEDER
RAPIDO CLINT STRIKES BACK

The Rockabye County series

THE SIXTEEN DOLLAR SHOOTER
THE LAWMEN OF ROCKABYE
  COUNTY
THE SHERIFF OF ROCKABYE
  COUNTY
THE PROFESSIONAL KILLERS
THE 1/4 SECOND DRAW
THE DEPUTIES
POINT OF CONTACT
THE OWLHOOT
RUN FOR THE BORDER
BAD HOMBRE
TEXAS TEAMWORK

Bunduki series

BUNDUKI
BUNDUKI AND DAWN
SACRIFICE FOR THE QUAGGA GOD
FEARLESS MASTER OF THE JUNGLE

Miscellaneous titles

J. T.'S HUNDREDTH
J. T.'S LADIES
MORE J. T.'S LADIES
J. T.'S LADIES RIDE AGAIN
IS-A-MAN (TEXAS WARRIOR)
WANTED! BELLE STARR (OKLAHOMA
  OUTLAW)*
SLAUGHTER'S WAY
TWO MILES TO THE BORDER
BLONDE GENIUS
(Written in collaboration with Peter
  Clawson)

*   Denotes title awaiting publication.
( )   Denotes position in which a proposed title will be placed.

OKLAHOMA OUTLAW

J.T. Edson

Formerly titled *Wanted! Belle Starr*

A DELL BOOK

Published by
Dell Publishing
a division of
Bantam Doubleday Dell Publishing Group, Inc.
1540 Broadway
New York, New York 10036

Formerly titled *Wanted! Belle Starr*

The trademark Dell® is registered in the U.S. Patent and Trademark Office.

ISBN: 0-440-22402-0

Reprinted by arrangement with Transworld Publishers Ltd.

Printed in the United States of America

Published simultaneously in Canada

December 1997

10 9 8 7 6 5 4 3 2 1

WCD

Dedicated to two of our favorite ladies, listed alphabetically for our protection: LIGHTNING, of British Gladiators, whose somersaults we could watch for hours, and MATILDA THE HUN, whose elfin grace, sylphlike agility, and strict adherence to the rules we so admired when she was a leading contender for Gorgeous Ladies of Wrestling.

AUTHOR'S NOTE

To save our "old hands" from repetition, but for the benefit of new readers, we have included details of the career and special qualifications of the Ysabel Kid, along with references to various Old West terms and events about which we are most frequently requested to supply extra information in the form of Appendices.

While we realize that in our present "permissive" society, we could include the actual profanities used by various people in the narrative, we do not concede that a spurious desire for "realism" is any excuse to do so.

Lastly, as we do not pander to the current "trendy" usage of the metric system, except in the events of referring to firearms where the caliber is generally given in millimeters—i.e., Walther P-38, 9mm—we will continue to employ miles, yards, feet, inches, pounds, and ounces when quoting distances and weights.

J.T. Edson,
Active Member, Western Writers of America,
Melton Mowbray,
Leics.,
England.

PART ONE

THE POISON AND THE CURE

1

MOST PAINFULLY DEAD

"*Indios bravos! Madre de Dios, senor,* your *Americano del Norte* 'Red'—don't you call them?—Indians are as *nothing* to frighten us. Not when in comparison with the kind of *Indios muy bravos* we have in the *Matto Grosso*. Unlike your Red Indians, they do not ride around openly to be shot at. No, they hide so very carefully and, before you even *suspect* they are there, they have started using their—how are you saying it?—'blowing pipes' and darts upon you."

There was a distinctly haughty disdain in the voice and demeanor of the speaker, who had been introduced to the other players in the poker game for high stakes as "Senora Donna Maria Constanza de la Santa Rosa." Black-haired, immaculately coiffured, olive-skinned, very beautiful, and with richly endowed feminine contours that her clothes emphasized—although not in a blatant manner—rather than concealed, her bearing was that of a person whose birthright and upbringing had placed her in a position of imperious authority. The low-crowned, round-brimmed black hat, dove-gray two-piece traveling costume, frilly-bosomed light blue silk blouse with a masculine black bow tie, and the jewelry sparkling around her neck, from her ears, on wrists and fingers, all indicated great wealth. To confirm this supposition, even before it had been supplemented by her frequent winnings, she had produced a considerable sum in the currency of the United States of America from the large black reticule that lay open on the table in front of her.

"Huh!" grunted the stocky and hard-featured man who—although his voice suggested he had been born and raised in the already notorious and less than salubrious Lower East Side district of New York City—had been presented before the start of the game as "Thomas Driberg," a cattle buyer from Chicago, Illinois. His clothing was that of a city dweller and his sallow complexion suggested such might be the case, but he had on a Western-style gunbelt with a walnut-handled Colt Civilian Model Peacemaker[1] in its fast-draw holster. "That don't seem so all-fired *dangerous* to me!"

"Ha, but this is only because you do not know *anything* about them, or their 'blowing pipes' and darts, senor," asserted the aristocratically arrogant beauty, her English good, albeit underlaid by a broad Spanish accent that enhanced the implication of Hispanic origins created by her name and appearance. "There is just one quick puff taken through a short hollow cane tube and you are stuck with a so-little spike of wood not thicker than a matchstick. Then, no matter how *quickly* you pull it out, unless you take the *only* anti-

---

1. *New readers can find information regarding the various types of Colt Model P "Single Action Army" revolver, more commonly called "the Peacemaker," in Footnote 1, APPENDIX ONE. J.T.E.*

dote—which is *very* rare and hard to come by—in no more than five minutes, you become most *painfully* dead without having seen, much less shot at, the man who has killed you."

"How?" inquired the tall, gaunt, and somberly clad man whose black and white attire, despite the fact that he was involved in a game of chance where considerable amounts of money were being bet, implied he was a member of the clergy.

"*Poison,* Fath—*Reverend* Huckfield," the beautiful young woman explained, making the substitution because she had discovered that the person she was addressing did not care to be referred to with the honorific more in keeping with the Catholic faith than that of his, as yet, unmentioned denomination. "A most *deadly* poison of a kind not widely known outside our country. As I told you, Manuel, my *husband*, is part *Matto Grosso Indio* and he knows of such things. He says it is called '*curare*'[2] and I have seen, with my own eyes, him kill a full-grown bull with the 'blowing pipe' and dart just as quickly as the men he has used it on for me have died."

Everything about the young man who was with her and whom she indicated by a casual wave of her bejeweled hand implied that, regardless of having been mentioned on more than one occasion as "Manuel, my *husband*"—in a tone that suggested more of an apology than pride—he was of a lower social status. Tall, slender, yet exuding an impression

---

2. Curare, *sometimes called "woorali," or "urare." A highly poisonous, blackish and brittle, resinous extract of certain South American trees of the genus* Strychnos, *particularly* S. Toxifera. *It is exceptionally fast acting and, by relaxing the "end plates" between the nerves and muscles, prevents the heart and lungs, from functioning, thereby causing death by asphyxiation, and is used by the native Indians to improve the lethal potential of their arrows. J.T.E.*

of wiry strength, his whole appearance gave credence to his being of mixed blood. Bareheaded, his
straight black hair hung down to shoulder level
and was held back by a headband of scarlet cloth.
However, with the exception of his eyes, there was
an almost babyishly innocent cast to his handsome,
Indian-dark features that did not seem in accord
with the possession of the lethal knowledge and
tendencies referred to by his wife. The eyes, a
curious red-hazel color, held a glint, even in repose,
that suggested the apparent innocence was not
necessarily indicative of his true nature. Sitting
ramrod straight in his chair, seemingly far from at
ease in such company, he conveyed the slightly
puzzled expression of one who knew he was the
subject of a comment in a language he could not
understand.

Regardless of the extreme affluence suggested by
the attire and jewelry of his wife, there was no such
elegance about Manuel. He wore a loose-fitting
light tan-colored waist-length leather jacket, an open-
necked and multihued cotton shirt such as was
sold cheaply in the trading posts of Indian reserva-
tions throughout the United States, and yellowish-
brown Nankeen trousers tucked into the legs of
low-heeled, but sharp-toed, black riding boots. A
massive, ivory-handled James Black bowie knife was
sheathed on the right side of his waist belt, which
was broad enough to support the far from inconsiderable weight, but he showed no sign of being
armed in any other way.

Only the Indian-dark young man seemed at odds
with the place in which the high-stakes game of
poker was being played. Although on the outskirts
of Newton, a town in Kansas depending for the
majority of its income upon the large herds of half-
wild longhorn cattle driven north from various parts

of Texas to its railroad pens,[3] the mansion and fittings of its sitting room had appointments equal to any in a larger Eastern city. Nor, Manuel excepted, did the players appear out of place in such a setting as far as their clothing, displayed wealth, and proclaimed occupations were concerned.

However, appearances can be deceptive!

Certainly nothing about the game of poker and its participants was what it seemed on the surface!

The events that had brought it about had commenced a few days earlier!

---

3. *Some of the events that led to such trail herds being delivered to the shipping pens of the railroad that passed through Kansas are recorded in* GOODNIGHT'S DREAM, FROM HIDE AND HORN, *and* SET TEXAS BACK ON HER FEET. *Further information regarding the handling of a trail drive being brought north from Texas is given in* TRAIL BOSS. *J.T.E.*

2

WHEN WILL I LEARN

"To hell with you and your goddamned tail-peddlers!" called the tallest of the three men who had emerged, with indications of having drunk "not wisely, but too well," from the side entrance at the insistence of the brawny bouncers employed by the Sunbird Saloon. Then, discovering they did not have the alley to themselves, he swung his gaze from the door that was being closed and went on in a lower voice, "Well now, just take a look at what's a-coming, Cousin Bert, Cousin Jubal. Ain't she just about the purtiest thing you ever did see?"

"I don't know about that, Cousin Henry," assessed "Cousin Bert," the second in height, his accent also indicating his birthright was in Illinois. "But she's sure enough close to being the *fanciest* I ever did see!"

"That's as may be," claimed "Cousin Jubal," his tone bitter and indicating that he too was from the "Sucker State," which was once the home of the late and great President Abraham Lincoln. "But I just bet she's reckoning's how she's a whole heap too good 'n' fancy for ordinary working fellers like *us*. 'Specially seeing we've been cheated out of all our hard-earned money in there 'n' can't afford to pay *her* nothing, neither, to act all friendly to us."

"I dunno," "Cousin Henry" growled, making no attempt to point out that the money was far from hard earned and had been spent legitimately in the saloon. "Could be we can sort of *talk* her into acting all friendly without getting paid nothing for it!"

"By golly, yes!" agreed the shortest, but no more prepossessing, member of the trio. "I reckon we might at that!"

"We won't never know 'less'n we give it a whirl," Cousin Bert supported. "So let's give her a whirl!"

Lordy lord! Belle Starr thought, studying the three men with range-wise eyes and listening to the remarks they were exchanging with no suggestion of wishing to avoid her hearing. She liked nothing of what she saw, or heard. Not only was she able to form a pretty accurate estimation of the kind they were, but she could also guess something of the reason for their comments. When *will* I learn not to go visiting dressed this way?

Tallish, lean, with long and straggly mouse-brown hair, there was a family likeness about the hollow-cheeked, unshaven and surly, drink-suffused features of the trio. Their attire might have led a person less knowing in Western matters to assume they were cowhands. Having grown up in the Indian Nations of Oklahoma, Belle had spent much of her life around "cow towns" and those that, like Newton, had come into being chiefly as shipping points from which the great trail herds out of Texas could be taken to the meat-hungry cities of the East. She knew such was *not* their occupation. The conclusion went beyond their Illinois accents. Other indications informed her they were unlikely to take any kind of employment requiring hard work, such as that of a cowhand. In all probability they earned their living via a willingness—if not exceptional skill—in making use of the low-tied Colt Peacemaker each was wearing. While they might not be rated among the top hands of that specialized field, she felt sure they could prove sufficiently dangerous under the prevailing conditions.

As a result of the deductions she had formed regarding the men, the lady outlaw was regretting the way in which she herself was behaving!

If there should be unwanted trouble, which seemed highly likely, Belle was ready to admit she had done much to bring it upon herself!

In spite of having become involved in a similar situation while she was visiting Ellsworth a few years earlier, Belle was dressed much as she had been then and she looked as if she could be a suitable candidate for being accosted in the manner that was intended by three men![1]

The bright orange-red shade of the hair visible beneath the lady outlaw's wide-brimmed and feather-decorated hat was not a color that would be sought by any "good" woman. Nor was the excessive makeup she had applied to her beautiful features, or the garish and—by the standards of the day—revealing clothing she had on, likely to be worn by a female member of the community unless she was employed in the cheaper varieties of the theatrical profession, a saloon, dance hall, or brothel.

Believing one or another such category was the status of their intended victim, the three men clearly considered she was offering a reasonably safe target to

---

1. *The events that led up to and followed the incident in Ellsworth, Kansas, are described in* CALAMITY, MARK AND BELLE. *J.T.E.*

vent the animosity that had been aroused by their having been justifiably evicted from the saloon. However, Belle was willing to concede they might not have behaved in a different fashion if she had presented an impression of frigid and righteous respectability. In their present state of drunken truculence, they were ripe for mischief without giving any thought to the possible consequences of their actions.

Unfortunately, the lady outlaw told herself as she was watching the trio spreading out to adopt a loose arrowhead formation across the width of the alley, there was no easy way to avoid their unwanted attentions!

Attempting verbal dissuasion would almost certainly prove a waste of time!

Too much noise was coming from the saloon to allow a scream for help to be heard before it was silenced by the men!

If Belle turned back, the trio would follow her into an even more deserted area than the alley!

The lady outlaw had a short-barreled Manhattan Navy revolver in the reticule that her left hand was grasping,[2] but she felt sure the mere sight of it would not be sufficient to frighten the men away. They had reached the state of intoxication when good sense and caution were forgotten. If she bought it out, she

---

2. *Resembling the Colt Navy Model of 1851, apart from having a spring plate interposed between the caps and the hammer, as produced by the manufacturers—who had long since gone out of business—the Manhattan Navy Model revolver had a barrel six and a half inches in length. The one carried by Belle Starr, when concealment was necessary, had had four and a half inches removed and the loading lever shortened accordingly. Should circumstances permit the wearing of a gunbelt and holster, she carried another that had not been modified in such a fashion. J.T.E.*

would almost certainly have to use it. While she would not have had any compunction over doing so as a last resource, this was a measure she had no desire to have forced upon her. Not only were the odds against her, three to one, but each was a professional gunfighter although they might fall short of being in the first string. Even if she should survive a shoot-out with them, unlikely as this was, she could cause the local peace officers to take a far greater interest in her than was desirable.

In fact, being in Newton as part of a tour of the trail-end towns in Kansas she was making with a small gang, carrying out a succession of lucrative confidence tricks, Belle was disinclined to create the kind of commotion that might bring the marshal or some of his deputies to investigate.

"Did you hear what Cousin Bert said, fancy-gal?" Jubal demanded, rather than merely inquired, glancing over his shoulder to ensure nobody was watching from the street at the front end of the alley. "How do you feel about getting all *friendly* with us good old boys when you ain't going to get paid?"

"Why, I surely can't think of *anything* I'd like to be doing *more*, sir," the lady outlaw lied, speaking with the accent of a well-educated Southron, which was her normal voice. She noticed that, although Henry had halted a short distance in front of her, the speaker and Bert were continuing to advance until on either side and just out of reaching distance. Showing no sign of her growing concern, she went on, "Only, I have a previous engagement with another gentleman of quality and just have to keep it."

"So you 'just have to,' do you?" Henry challenged, mimicking Belle's way of speaking, his whole bearing redolent of menace as he stood with hands on hips and feet spread apart. Resuming his normal half-snarling, half-whining tone, he continued. "Well, me 'n' my cousins just don't see it that way, you 'mother something,'[3] highfalutin, peckerwood tail-peddler!"[4]

"You, *sir*," Belle said, with a mildness she was far from feeling, "are no *gentleman* to be using such language!"

While delivering the sentiment, the lady outlaw was taking hold of and drawing the front of her skirt to above knee level. Doing so did not exhibit the kind of underclothing that might have been expected to supplement such garish and revealing outer garments. High heeled and comparatively dainty though they might be, the black riding boots she was displaying were clearly functional rather than decorative. Nor were the figure-hugging white riding breeches tucked into their Hessian legs any more conventional attire.

Before any of the trio could draw conclusions from what was being exposed to their gaze, in the light of the lantern hanging above the side door of the saloon, Belle's shapely right leg rose swiftly!

Henry could hardly have selected a posture better suited to the purpose of the lady outlaw. In fact, due to the speed with which the kick was delivered and the impediment to her movements created by the rucked-up skirt, he might have considered himself fortunate that she was prevented from employing her full strength. Not that he devoted any thought to the matter when the foot reached its intended target. Taken at the most vulnerable point of the masculine anatomy, he could do nothing more constructive than let out a strangled gasp of agony and stumble away from his assailant with both hands going to the stricken area.

---

3. *See* Paragraph Three *of our* AUTHOR's NOTE. *J.T.E.*

4. *"Peckerwood tail-peddler"*: *derogatory name for a prostitute who was a Southron. J.T.E.*

Bringing down her foot, Belle used it as a pivot upon which to turn toward Bert. Grasping the reticule in both hands, she swung it so as to use the revolver it concealed as an improvised club. Already springing toward her with hands rising to reach and grab hold, he walked into the blow. Unfortunately for her, circumstances were against her being able to produce the full effects with her, of necessity, hurried movements. While the attack landed sufficiently hard to hurt and cause the approaching fingers to miss their selected target, it failed to render him even close to *hors de combat* as she had intended.

Caught just as unawares by the speed and skill with which their proposed victim was responding, Jubal nevertheless had started acting in a way that helped his second cousin. With his right hand catching her by the shoulder as she was turning, his left sank into the top of the wide-brimmed hat. While he failed to stop the blow with the reticule being delivered, he had helped to reduce its impact somewhat.

Just as he was commencing to haul Belle away from Bert, Jubal felt the hat coming off in his grasp. Much to his further amazement, he found he was removing the orange-red "hair" at the same time. Startled by the discovery that he was apparently scalping his captive without first having even used a knife to sever the skin around the head, he could not prevent her from snatching free her shoulder. A moment later, her left elbow was rammed into his solar plexus with some force. Giving vent to a grunt of pain, he was driven backward with the hat and well-made wig falling from his hands. Swinging around, her excessively made-up face appearing incongruous when taken with the exposure of her short-cropped brunette hair,[5] her right fist landed a hard punch to his jaw.

Once again, the lady outlaw was not allowed to make the most of the advantage she had gained!

Halting the involuntary stagger caused by the blow from the reticule, Bert sprang forward to wrap his arms around Belle. Caught from the rear, with hands pinioned to her sides, she knew her position was rapidly becoming desperate. Face darkened and made even more ugly by rage, Henry was starting to advance. It was obvious to her that, even if at first he might have been gentler with her because she was a woman, now he would not be deterred from delivering a brutal attack by considerations of her sex.

Struggling against the encircling arms of the man behind her, unable to force them apart by sheer strength, the lady outlaw tried to escape by driving the back of her close-cropped head into his face. Prevented from achieving this by the brim of his hat, she also prepared to try to kick away the other attacker as he was already approaching. She did not hold out much hope for her chances when she made the attempt.

All in all, Belle considered she was in as dire a strait as at almost any other time in her eventful young life!

---

5. *As we pointed out in* WACO's BADGE, *although we had not previously known it, Belle Starr had the habit of having her hair cut short when engaged upon criminal activities that required her to make frequent changes to her appearances by adopting disguises. Belle "the Rebel Spy" Boyd— some details of whose career are given in various volumes of the* Civil War *and* Floating Outfit *series—used a similar hairstyle while serving with first the Confederate, hence her sobriquet, and then the United States Secret Service. J.T.E.*

3

YOU'RE LUCKIER'N YOU KNOW

Before either Belle Starr or Henry could put
their respective intentions into effect, there was an
interruption!

Having been passing the front entrance to the alley
between the Sunbird Saloon and the gunsmith's shop
next door—the latter already closed for the night—a
tall, well-built, blond-haired, and good-looking young
man was attracted by the commotion. Clad in a tan-
colored flat cloth cap, gray Norfolk jacket, white shirt
with an attachable celluloid collar, dark green and
blue striped necktie, knickerbocker trousers, tartan
woolen socks, and untanned walking boots, but showing no sign of being armed, he was more likely to be
from the East than a Westerner. Seeing what was happening, he immediately turned to the rescue.

"Hey!" the blond shouted, as he started to run
along the alley. His accent proved to be that of a well-
educated New Englander as he went on, "Take your
hands off that young woman!"

Well-intentioned though the motives of the newcomer undoubtedly were and most welcome, the lady outlaw considered he was ill-advised to have announced his presence in such a fashion!

For all that, aided by the speed at which he was moving, the blond achieved some success, in spite of having deprived his arrival of the element of surprise!

Grabbing Henry by the shoulders before he could turn, the Easterner flung him aside. Jubal, on the point of returning to help deal with the beautiful young woman held by Bert, had his attention attracted by the indiscreet demand. He changed direction and lunged forward. Adopting the posture of a participant in the fast-developing sport of boxing with gloves and timed rounds, instead of fighting barehanded until one combatant was knocked down, the blond met the attack competently enough. Deftly blocking the blow being swung at him with his left hand, he sent the right in a stylish jab to the face. Bringing a trickle of blood from the top lip and snapping back the head, the punch caused its recipient to retreat a few hurried steps and his assailant went after him with the intention of delivering a coup de grâce.

Effective as such methods might have been in the boxing ring of an Eastern sporting club against another amateur opponent engaged in a friendly bout, they proved to be less efficacious for a roughhouse brawl in a Kansas trail-end town with more than one antagonist involved.

Hurling Belle so that she collided with the wall of the gunsmith's shop and was momentarily stunned, Bert sprang at and trapped the young man in the same manner he had employed to reduce her ability to fight back. Snarling curses, the other cousins—Henry having recovered sufficiently from the kick to join in—diverted their rage from her to the newcomer and converged with the intention of venting it upon him.

Once again, the trio were to be thwarted!

However, on this occasion, the intervention was by somebody whose views on sporting conduct were clearly better attuned to the needs of the situation!

Clad in all-black clothing, of the style that was practically *de rigueur* for a cowhand from Texas, except that his sharp-toed boots had low heels, the most recent arrival upon the scene was tall, with a whipcord slender build and Indian-dark, almost babyishly handsome features that made him appear very young. Dangling suspended by its *barbiquejo* chin strap on his shoulders, his hat left exposed glossy black hair that had recently been cut to an acceptable shortness. Regardless of his facial appearance, unlike his predecessor, he was not without visible weapons. On the contrary, he was remarkably well-armed. The Winchester Model of 1873 rifle he was carrying, its finish being of a much higher grade than that given to standard production pieces, was augmented by an old Colt Dragoon Model of 1848 revolver, butt forward in the holster on the right side of his gunbelt, and an ivory-handled James Black bowie knife of massive dimensions in a sheath at the left.

Advancing swiftly and silently, the young Texan made no attempt to announce his presence in any way until he was close enough to do so with most effect. Even then, he did not speak. Instead, he delivered a round arm swing that slammed the twenty-six-inch octagonal barrel of the rifle against the side of Henry's head. The impact twirled the tallest of the cousins toward the wall of the saloon. Striking and rebounding from the unyielding planks, he went down in the limp and uncaring fashion of one who had been rendered unconscious.

Seeing what happened to Henry, Jubal forgot his intention of repaying the punch he had taken from the New Englander. Instead, he started to reach for his holstered Colt and began to turn upon the latest arrival. Without so much as having broken stride while felling the tallest cousin, holding the rifle with only his right hand grasping the wrist of the butt— disregarding the fact that it was not an ordinary production model, but one of the rare "One of a Thousand" type so highly prized and much sought after on account of their superlative quality—he continued to use it as a club rather than a firearm. Reversing the direction it was traveling, the barrel swept around just as rapidly and arrived with an equal force against Jubal's jaw before the draw was completed. He was sent in a headlong plunge against the other building, from which he flopped to sprawl unmoving on the ground.

Alarmed by the unexpected and decidedly disturbing way in which the affair was developing, Bert shoved the New Englander forward and also elected to continue the hostilities with his revolver. As he was reaching for it, Belle lurched from where she had been flung and rammed shoulder first into his back. He was sent after the young man he had pushed in the direction of the black-dressed Texan, but was not offered an opportunity to halt what he sensed to be a most undesirable movement.

Stepping aside with the casual-seeming ease of a master toreador avoiding the charge of an inexperienced bull, the second rescuer took himself clear of the blond and into view of the last cousin. Catching the wooden foregrip of the Winchester with his left hand, he lunged as if he were a soldier delivering an attack with a bayonet. Jabbed just below the breastbone with the muzzle of the weapon, all the breath left Bert's lungs in an agonized "whoosh!" As he was stumbling away and all thoughts of pulling the Colt were obliterated, the rifle was brought up to hook beneath his descending jaw. Giving a surging heave, indicative of the powerful muscles of the slender frame, the Texan lifted and flung him backward. His head slammed against the ground and he, too, lapsed into immobility.

"Now I wouldn't want to go sounding all pushy and nosy afore we've so much's said, 'Howdy, you-all,' formal-like, Mr. Bullstrode," remarked the Indian-dark and most effective young intruder, his Texas drawl a musical tenor, having glanced around to ensure there was no further need for hostile action against the trio. "But, happen you're figuring on staying out west of the Big Muddy and aim to keep billing in on other folks' doings, no matter should it be thought polite back to home, I wouldn't keep on shouting to let them know you're coming for 'em, head down 'n' horns a-hooking."

"*Lon!*" Belle exclaimed before the New Englander could reply to what she considered was excellent advice, pausing as she was bending to retrieve the hat and wig. "*Lon Ysabel.* Well, I'll be damned if it isn't *you!*"

"Well, now," replied the Ysabel Kid, showing none of the surprise he was experiencing over the lady whom he and the young Easterner had rescued. "There's some might say's how you'll be damned 'most any ways it's taken."

"I've heard the same thing said about *you* and with *better* reason," the lady outlaw claimed, noticing that the young Texan had not given any suggestion of knowing her true identity. Picking up and starting to replace her dislodged property, the hat being secured by a pin to the wig, she went on, "But I'll give you *one* thing. You boys of Ole Devil's floating outfit surely know how to come to hand when you're most badly needed."

"That's been said so often, it must be truthful true," the Kid asserted, with a spurious modesty he knew would be expected by the beautiful young woman. "Only this time, I'd say you're luckier'n you know."

"How come?" Belle inquired.

"We should've got here two, three days back," the Texan explained, directing the words to the New Englander as much as the lady outlaw. "Which's how-all I got to be on hand right now. Cap'n Fog's sent me on ahead to let you know's how he's on his way in, Mr. Bullstrode. The desk clerk down to the hotel told me's you'd just gone out 'n' who to look for. Trouble being, just afore I could catch up and say, 'Howdy, you'all,' I saw you headed in here at a rush and concluded I'd best come see what was doing."

"I'm pleased you did," Andrew Bullstrode declared, but a note of bitterness came into his voice as he continued, "Only, I wish Captain Fog could have got here on time, because I've made a goddamned fool of myself while I was waiting."

"How come!" the Kid inquired.

"I met a young woman at the hotel—!" the New Englander began, too miserable to hold back the confession he knew he would eventually be compelled to make elsewhere, even though he was in the presence of strangers.

"How about telling us what happened while we're *walking?*" Belle suggested, her manner sympathetic. "I'd rather not stay here until the marshal or some of his deputies come to find out why those three knob-heads have been treated so rough."

"Or me, comes to that," the Kid supported, being sufficiently well acquainted with the lady outlaw to understand her disinclination to be interviewed by the local peace officers. "The John Laws in this town aren't a bunch of Kansas fighting pimps like those goddamned Earp boys, but they don't take kind' to having fellers whomped about so cruel, no matter why it's dont. I know we-all had right good cause to whomp 'em, but I'd sooner not spend the time it'll take telling the why of it."

"But—!" Bullstrode began, his upbringing in the best part of Newark, New Jersey, having imbued a strong sense of respect for law and order that led him to consider the proposal far from ethical.

"From what you've told us so far, my guess is that the sooner we hear the rest of your story the better," the lady outlaw claimed. "And we won't be able to do that while the marshal or his deputies are questioning us, even if you wanted *them* to hear what you have to say. On top of which, I've got what I reckon to be pretty sound reasons for not wanting to give them a chance to talk to *me*."

"I'm going to walk along with 'Miss Beauregard' for a spell," the Kid declared, in a tone that brooked no argument, having deduced from the disguise that Belle would not want her true identity revealed and employing one of her favourite aliases. "And, going by what you started to say, I've got a sneaky feeling you're sort of caught 'tween a rock and a hard place. Which being, I reckon you'd best come and tell us all about it."

4

HE LET HIMSELF BE TAKEN

"You're certainly right in assuming I'm in trouble," Andrew Bullstrode confessed, as he was accompanying Belle Starr and the Ysabel Kid in the direction from which, unbeknownst to him, she had entered the alley. Feeling a desperate need to talk to somebody, the further realization that the Indian-dark young Texan would have to be told what had happened was giving him all the inducement necessary to do so. "I met this young woman in the dining room at the hotel while I was having dinner last night and, seeing she looked somewhat distressed, got to talking with her. She finally told me, after some prompting, she was in difficulty because her brother had lost a lot of money in a game of poker—!"

"She's about my height," the lady outlaw interposed, bringing the explanation to a halt as the New Englander glanced at her in a doubtful fashion. "A real pretty blonde, unless she's changed its color, who looks like butter wouldn't melt in her mouth. Seeing that I'm not inclined to be *catty*—well, not *especially*—I'll say she's *willowly* in build and not skinny."

"Yes, she is!" the blond-haired young man gasped, swinging his gaze rapidly toward the speaker instead of giving his attention to the Kid. "But how—?"

"And," the lady outlaw went on, as if the interruption to her description had never been made. "Because her brother had had to leave town earlier that afternoon, she wanted you to go along with her to hand over payment for an i.o.u. he'd signed to cover his losses."

"Why, *yes*, that's exactly how it was!" Bullstrode exclaimed, staring practically goggle-eyed at the young woman he had assumed to be nothing more than a less-than-respectable acquaintance of the black-clad Texan. "But how did you *know*?"

"Then, on the way to the game, which her 'brother' had assured her was completely honest, she found out you reckoned yourself a better-than-fair poker player," Belle continued, without supplying the information that had been requested. "After which, she suggested you should use her savings and try to win back at least some of the money he'd lost and, with her being so sweet, innocent and defenseless to look at, you were enough of the gallant gentleman to give it a whirl. Only, instead of getting back her 'brother's' money, you lost all she'd given you and, in trying to get that back, got through all of your own."

"I don't know how *you* know, but that's just the way it happened!" Bullstrode admitted, hoping he was not sounding and looking as big a fool as he felt while listening to a surprisingly accurate description of the previous night's events. Realizing there must be vastly more to the beautiful and garishly dressed young woman than appeared upon the surface, certainly that she was something vastly different from what he had taken her for—although he could not envisage her exact status—he went on in a voice redolent of the misery and shame he had been experiencing all day, "Except that it wasn't just my own money I lost!"

"Do tell," the Kid drawled in what seemed a disinterested manner and was, in fact, considered as being by the New Englander. The Kid had sensed that the final words of the confession were intended more for him than the lady outlaw. "So this skinny li'l gal and her good buddies took you for all the cash you were sent here to pass on to Ole Devil, huh?"

"Every last cent of it!" Bullstrode confirmed, his voice scarcely louder than a whisper. "God, I was such a *fool*!"

"Well, yes, it sounds like you just could've been at that," the Texan asserted, but his demeanor gave little or no indication of how he was receiving the news that the large sum of money intended for his employer, General Jackson Baines "Ole Devil" Hardin, had been lost in a game of poker. "Thing being, was you cheated?"

"I think I must have been," the New Englander answered. "But I can't imagine how they did it. Everything seemed straight and aboveboard."

"It 'most always does, happen them doing the taking're good enough," the Kid declared. "How'd they take you?'

"Almost all of it went on the final pot," Bullstrode replied, quietly and with the bitterness of desperation. "I was holding four jacks and an ace dealt pat, and everybody else drew at least two cards. The betting was pretty heavy until, at last, only Reverend Huckfield and I were left."

"*Reverend* Huckfield?" the Kid queried.

"That's how he was introduced to me," the New Englander confirmed. "I've known other members of the clergy who like to gamble for high stakes and, him being in the game, I felt sure it must be honest."

"Most folks would have felt the same," Belle commiserated, as the explanation was brought to an embarrassed end. "That's why the *Reverend* Huckfield was sitting in. So how did the play go?"

"He'd taken three cards on the draw," Bullstrode explained, at last having accepted, instead of trying to fight off the belief, that he had been taken in by a well-devised and -executed plot. "And, as I'd seen a queen and a couple of kings thrown in when the others folded, I couldn't see how I could possibly be beaten by any hand he'd filled."

"You were counting on him having drawn three cards to a pair," the lady outlaw suggested, the young man having paused and glanced her way as if wondering whether she was able to follow the description of the events. "Which, even if he had caught the other two, they wouldn't be able to beat your four jacks as they couldn't be queens, kings, or aces."

"That's how *anybody* would have seen it!" the New Englander claimed, with justification. "Particularly after the right and cagey game he'd been playing."

"But he still topped your four jacks with a straight flush on the showdown," the lady outlaw stated rather than guessed.[1]

"You're right," Bullstrode conceded, surprised at finding his confession was being accepted without any sign of derision or condemnation on the part of the beautiful if over-made-up woman and the very young-seeming Texan (whom he now suspected was somewhat older and far more worldly than appearances suggested). Feeling slightly better now that he had admitted what he had come to realize had been very foolish behavior, he elaborated, "I did think he was

---

1. *An explanation of the relative value of the "hands" in the game of poker is given in* TWO MILES TO THE BORDER. *J.T.E.*

drawing to improve a pair, the same way he had several times before. Nobody but the rankest 'lamb' or 'rabbit' would have stayed in a pot that steep and drawn three cards in the hope of filling a straight flush, and although I wouldn't have rated him as any kind of poker playing 'wolf,' he'd played a whole lot smarter than that up until then."

"All of which was intended to get you thinking you *couldn't* lose the pot," Belle went on, as the New Englander stopped speaking. "So you saw what you took to be your chance to get back all the money you and dear Emily—if that's the name she gave you—and her poor 'brother' had lost, perhaps with some more on top of it. The trouble was, the only way you could stay in the pot was by putting up that ten thousand dollars you were supposed to deliver to Dusty Fog for General Hardin."

"Yes, that h—!" Bullstrode began, before the full import of what had just been said struck him. Swinging his startled gaze to the lady outlaw, he demanded not without a noticeable trace of suspicion, "How do you know it was *ten thousand* dollars?"

"I heard all about it and you just after I arrived in town," Belle replied, but refrained from mentioning that when she had discovered for whom the money was intended it had caused her to rule out the young New Englander as one of her own possible victims. A friendship of long standing with Ole Devil Hardin's floating outfit, and not a fear of the consequences, which would have deterred most Western criminals, had led her to reach her decision. This, in addition to considering herself under an obligation to him for his attempt in helping her against the three drunken cousins, made her go on. "The thing is, how do we go about getting it and your money back from them?"

"Well, now," the Kid drawled and, regardless of the seemingly gentle way in which he was speaking, something in his manner caused Bullstrode to eye him uneasily. "Happen they're still around town, I could maybe drift along and *ask* them real friendly-like to give it back to you."

"They're still in town," the New Englander claimed, in response to the interrogative glances directed his way by his companions. "At least, they were this morning. The Duke of Haute-Savoie was with Reverend Huck-field when he came to collect his winnings. I haven't seen either of them, or the girl, since then. But two of the other men who were playing went out of the hotel earlier this evening."

"That means they're still around," the lady outlaw estimated, not without satisfaction. "They'll have been keeping watch on you all day to find out whether you had got suspicious and meant to tell the marshal what had happened."

"I thought of doing just that," Bullstrode stated grimly. "But the game took place in one of the big mansions on the edge of town, and with the quality of the people who were playing, I kept telling myself I must be wrong and hadn't been cheated. At least, I couldn't have told the marshal I'd seen *anything* to make me believe I'd been other than outsmarted fairly."

"You're lucky you didn't try to go and tell about them. They'd have stopped you cold," Belle asserted. "As it is, you were their first 'mark' here, and after the expense they'll have gone to hiring that house, they're likely to be staying a few more days to pick up another couple or so."

"Which being," the black-dressed Texan said, in the same apparently mild tone and looking almost angelically innocent, "should you just tell me where they're at, I'll drift on over and say, 'Howdy, you-all.' "

"And, seeing they're trampling on *my* range and have already wide-looped one mark I was fixing to slap my brand on—not you, Mr. Bullstrode, but back along the railroad a piece—I'd say go to it, Lon," the lady outlaw declared, having no illusions regarding the true nature of the Ysabel Kid.[2] "Doing it your *Pehnane* Commanche way could get back the money, I'll admit—!"

"But?" the Texan prompted.

"But not without you winding up having to explain to the marshal why you took to the warpath," Belle elaborated. "Which, unless I'm mistaken, is the last thing Mr. Bullstrode wants when it means that the story of how he let himself be taken will be spread around. It won't just stay hereabouts, should that happen."

"You're right about *that*, 'Miss Beauregard'!" the New Englander affirmed vehemently. In a quieter tone, he continued, "I know I haven't shown in any too good a light by what I've done, but to have word of it get back home will ruin whatever chances I have of making a career for myself."

"That's what I thought," Belle admitted, with genuine sympathy and understanding.

"I still can't believe the girl was in it!" Bullstrode said. "She looked so young and innocent—!"

"And isn't *either*," the lady outlaw interrupted. She was all too aware—although she tended to select quarry less likely to seek revenge by informing the law-enforcement agencies, because they'd be hard put to explain their own motives in seeking a big gambling game—of how easily a lonely and susceptible young man could be taken in by a woman with the looks and histrionic abilities of the blonde she had described. Then her gaze swung to the Texan and she went on, "Your way is out, Lon."

---

2. *Details of the family background and special qualifications of the Ysabel Kid are given in* APPENDIX TWO. *J.T.E.*

"Do you have something better in mind?" the Kid inquired, although his attitude suggested he felt sure this was the case.

"Not so much better as less direct," Belle replied. "In fact, it's going to need to be a real sneaky way to get the money back."

5

A SUBJECT LESS GRUESOME

"*Sacre bleu*, how absolutely *horrible*!" gasped Emily Chauvelin, who was currently using as an alias the title "the Duchess of Haute-Savoie." Fitting the description given to Andrew Bullstrode by Belle Starr, tastefully and expensively dressed and bejeweled, her English had a French accent that was somewhat less pronounced than the Spanish timbre employed by her intended victim. Darting a glance close to revulsion at the longhaired and Indian-dark young man credited with very deadly knowledge, she gave a shiver and went on, "Can't we talk of something less *frightful*, please?"

"Perhaps you will cut the cards for me, please, Donna Maria?" requested Armond, "Duke of Haute-Savoie," whose English was of much the same quality as the woman who was his wife in real life, although she occasionally posed in other capacities. Of medium height, stocky in build, black haired and swarthily handsome, with a sharp-pointed mustache and tiny chin beard in the Gallic fashion, he too was immaculately dressed.

Having completed the shuffling of the deck during the description of how fatally effective a "blowing pipe" and its darts tipped with *curare* could be, he held it toward Belle Starr. "Like *mon cher* Emily, I too feel a change to a subject less *gruesome* would be welcome."

"Yeah, verily," intoned "Reverend" Leslie Huckfield, as somberly as if delivering a sermon for the wealthy and influential local congregation he had claimed to represent. "Though the ways of the ungodly are indeed mysterious, I agree they do not make a pleasant topic of conversation."

"But of course," the lady outlaw assented, in the manner of one conferring a favor. "I was only explaining for Senor Driberg."

After Belle had left to start making her preparations for the attempt to retrieve Andrew Bullstrode's money on the night of their meeting, the young man had expressed doubts over whether she would be able to accomplish anything. Neither she nor the Ysabel Kid had told him of her true identity.

But, being far better informed, the Indian-dark young Texan had not suffered from any such lack of confidence!

Subsequent events had proved the faith shown by the Kid to be fully justified!

Having put to good use her specialized knowledge, facilities, and talent, the lady outlaw had been able to supply everything she considered would be needed for the scheme she had concocted.

The first thing arranged by Belle was for the young New Englander to make it appear he had left Newton, rather than stay around admitting he had allowed himself to be cheated out of the money put in his care. Although he had not been under observation on the evening when they had become acquainted, the surveillance was resumed the following morning. He had been followed to the railroad depot by Driberg and another member of the gang, then watched while boarding an eastbound train. Ostensibly returning home, his misgivings having to some extent been dispelled by the confidence in her expressed by the Kid after they had separated the previous night—still, however, without having learned who she was—he had carried out her instructions by going only as far as the next town along the tracks.

Nor had Bullstrode traveled alone, Belle and the Kid having joined him on the train when satisfied none of the gang were traveling in it to ensure he did not change his mind. Shortly after their arrival at the point of disembarkation, a telegraph from one of the lady outlaw's associates had confirmed in a simple code that the ploy was successful. Obviously satisfied that their latest dupe had refrained from lodging a complaint with the local peace officers, and also would not be around to warn others, everything indicated the gang were remaining in Newton to acquire further victims. They would be kept under observation, nevertheless, in case they should leave before she returned. If this had happened, steps would have been taken to find out their next destination.

Staining her skin the olive brown of a Latin, and equipping herself with appropriate wig and clothing, Belle had transformed herself into "Senora Donna Maria Constanza de la Santa Rosa." Her pose was that of an extremely wealthy and headstrong South American who was visiting the Kansas trail-end towns with her "husband," prior to going farther west on a hunting trip, and to meet ranchers from Texas and arrange to purchase cattle for her *estancia* in Brazil. It was a character she had played in the past and, although unable to speak Portuguese—the main language of that country—she could tell a sufficiently convincing story to explain how a person of "Spanish" birthright came to be living there. She also knew enough to be able to satisfy the curiosity of anyone who had not been to or made an extensive study of Brazil and its customs.

On learning how the lady outlaw was planning to handle the retrieval, being aware that it would not be achieved without considerable risk, the Kid had insisted upon posing as her "husband." Although he was not trained as a confidence trickster, knowing his capabilities in other fields, she had concluded he was better suited to play the role she envisaged than any member of her "crew." He was also less likely to be recognized, as the rest of her gang were all well-known to other "bunco steerers." She had therefore given her concurrence.

Despite the Texan having his black hair cut short after the fashion of cowhands, among whom the possession of long locks and bushy beards was an abomination, he had only needed an easily provided suitable wig and clothing to complete his disguise. He was already sufficiently dark-skinned and his Spanish was fluent enough for Belle to pass him as her part Indian *gaucho* husband, brought from another property her family owned in Agrentina. He had been helped in the portrayal by ostensibly being unable to speak or understand English as well as—if necessary—Portuguese. Having been less certain of his ability as an actor than a fighting man, she had considered it was advisable to restrict the amount he had to do and had taken the main burden of creating the desired effect upon herself. Nor, having conceded his limitations, had he raised any objections to the arrangements.

Leaving Bullstrode behind, the lady outlaw and the Texan had returned by train to Newton in their disguises. They had been followed from the depot to the best hotel by Thomas Driberg. Having established themselves in the finest suite, demanding it with the imperious and impressive attitude of one used to having her own way in everything, Belle had set about giving the impression that she liked to gamble. They had not had a long wait before the bait was taken.

Earlier that evening, introducing themselves as the "Duchess and Duke of Haute-Savoie, from Paris, France," the couple responsible for fleecing the young New Englander had insisted upon taking the "other foreign visitors" to dinner in the hotel's dining room. During the meal, they had expressed sympathy with "Donna Maria" when she complained that ladies like herself were not allowed into the barroom to join a game of poker. Saying they had arranged for a few acquaintances to play at the house they were renting, as Emily was subject to the same annoying restriction in the town's places of entertainment, Armond Chauvelin had offered to let their "newfound friends" go with them and participate.

Visiting the ladies' rest room before leaving the hotel, Belle had given Emily an "explanation" of the Kid's status and presence. Admitting that he was "far below her class" and hoping he would never learn what she had said, she had attributed him with sexual prowess of a high order. The impression she created was that his position was less that of an equal partner in a matrimonial alliance than a combined traveling companion, bedmate, and bodyguard. With regard to the latter, she had claimed he was most effective. However, sharing a general belief that she ascribed to all *gauchos*, that the harder one pulled the trigger, the faster the bullet flew, she said he was no gunfighter. Instead, he relied upon the big bowie knife and other, even more deadly, methods—which she did not elaborate upon at that time—if there should be the need to protect her. When "the Duchess" had suggested she leave him behind, clearly having felt concerned over having such a potentially dangerous person along, she had declared this was unwise, as his weakness for hard liquor and sexual proclivities made it necessary for her to keep him under constant observation. Finding "Donna Maria" was adamant upon the matter, Emily had given grudging consent to "Manuel" accompanying them.

Taken to the luxuriously furnished mansion in the most wealthy section of Newton, rented from the butler and housekeeper while the owners were away on vacation, the lady outlaw and the Texan had found everything pretty much as described by Bullstrode. One problem the Kid had anticipated had not arisen. Although she was known to the dishonest employees, as she had admitted, she had also been aware that neither would be on the premises. One of the conditions the servants had imposed when engaging in their transaction was that they would be absent at all times the property was in use. This offered them an excuse to plead ignorance if their "guests" should be caught.

The only major difference in the setup was that, having no need to act as lure for a susceptible young man, Emily was serving in her true capacity as Armond Chauvelin's wife. All the "acquaintances" were the same and using the supposed occupations they had given to their previous victim.

What was more, the pattern of the play had followed a similar course!

With the Kid seated by her side, but not playing due to the supposed language difficulty, Belle had quickly established that she had no liking for losing. Then, although she had played with far less skill than she actually possessed, she had been allowed to win steadily. However, the attempts made by Emily to ply her and the Texan with hard liquor had met with no success. Claiming almost total abstinence for herself, she had asserted that—as she had heard was also the case with Indians and half-breeds in North America—

it was most unwise to let "Manuel" drink intoxicating beverages.

Commenting upon the proposed "hunting trip," apparently because she was in high spirits over having taken another sizable pot—which she had felt sure was presented to her, despite Driberg having held a hand of higher value than the one she displayed—the lady outlaw had been offered the opening she needed to introduce a subject essential to the culmination of her scheme.

"As you wish, Armond, Fath—*Reverend*," Belle continued, with the good-humored acquiescence of a person who found everything was going as she desired. Which was true, although not in the way the majority of her audience believed to be the case. She was most gratified by the way in which all the members of the gang were studying the Kid in a speculative, even perturbed fashion. "Let us by all means play on, so I can make the most of my good fortune!'

"You're real *lucky*, and that's a fact!" Driberg admitted, with the sourness of a disgruntled loser. "There's none of us can do a thing right against you!"

6

ALL THINGS ARE POSSIBLE

"Madre de Dios!" Belle Starr gasped, the game having been resumed and two more pots coming her way without any suggestion the trap had begun to be sprung. Glancing at the grandfather clock in the corner of the room, while the deck was being shuffled in what she knew to be a legitimate fashion, she continued, "Is that the hour?"

"It is," Armond Chauvelin confirmed, a trace of suspicion in his otherwise blandly polite voice. "Why?"

"Much as I hate to do so while enjoying such a *lucky* streak, I'm afraid I must leave after your next deal, my dear Armond," the lady outlaw explained. "I have the so early meeting in the morning with a Captain *Dusty* Fog—what strange names these *Americanos del Norte* have, don't you think?"

"*Very* strange," the "Duke of Haute-Savoie" agreed, his tone pensive as he was aware of the reputation ascribed to the man mentioned by his intended victim. He found the possibility of her attending such a meeting disturbing.[1] "Do you know him well?"

"I have heard something about him, but we have never met," Belle replied, truthfully with the first part and much less so where the second was concerned. "By all accounts, he is segundo for an uncle who owns one of the largest ranches in Texas and should be able to offer me many cattle at a suitable price. We are to discuss this in the morning, and I *never* care to talk the business unless I am fully rested."

"A most sensible precaution, *mon cher* Donna Maria," Chauvelin praised jovially, concluding there was no justification for his fear that the beautiful young woman was intending to make an excuse and leave before the trap could be sprung. He also decided, bearing in mind the person she was meeting in the morning, that it would be advisable to leave Newton after the game was over. Turning his gaze to his wife and giving a brief inclination of his head, receiving an equally quick nod indicating an understanding of what was wanted, he went on, "But perhaps your luck will change before you leave us."

"All things are *possible*," Belle conceded, giving no indication of having noticed the exchange of signals between her host and hostess. "That is what gives gambling its fascination for me. However, as I have been so lucky all evening, I'm sure my good fortune will last a little longer and I hope you won't object to me leaving a winner?"

"Certainly not," Chauvelin lied, considering such a contingency was nonexistent. "The chance of winning, or even *losing*, is what gives gambling its fascination for me also. By the way, Mr. Driberg, are you acquainted with Captain Fog?"

---

1. *Information regarding how the reputation was acquired by Captain Dustine Edward Marsden "Dusty" Fog, C.S.A., can be found in various volumes of the* Civil War *and* Floating Outfit *series. Something of his connection with the Ysabel Kid is described in* APPENDIX TWO. *J.T.E.*

"I've bought cattle from him," the stocky and hard-featured man replied, guessing what was expected of him. "Now, there's a feller who enjoys a game of poker. I'll say one thing about him, though. He surely hates a poor loser and's told me more than once he wouldn't do business with one under no circumstances."

"How *interesting*," the "Duke" declared, hoping the point would be taken by "Donna Maria Constanza de la Santa Rosa" and prevent her from complaining about her losses to the Texan when they met the following morning.

"Hey, 'Mrs. Duke,' ma'am," Thomas Driberg went on, knowing what was required of him at this point in the proceedings. "Would there be any chance of me and the boys getting drinks before the next pot?"

"Verily," supported "Reverend" Leslie Huckfield. "For does it not say in the Good Book, 'Take a little wine for your stomach'?"

"Of course," Emily Chauvelin assented. "If you will tell me what drinks you want, I will go and start preparing them right away. Perhaps, Donna Maria, as you are to leave us so soon, we might persuade you and your husband to join us this time?"

"But of course," the lady outlaw replied, with the air of one so satisfied by the way things were going she could afford to be magnanimous. However, she had fully intended to request that she and the Ysabel Kid were included if the invitation had not been forthcoming. "We certainly will and, as it will be only the *one*, 'Manuel' will only be affected *properly* by it." Directing a knowing glance at the "Duchess" as she was making the last part of the statement, she went on, "We will each have a glass of wine, please."

As she had on other occasions when a "guest" had made a similar request for liquid refreshment, Emily disappeared into the kitchen. She had already explained to Belle that the servants had all been given the evening off to avoid embarrassment for "Reverend" Huckfield—whose congregation, it was claimed, would not approve of him playing poker for any kind of stakes even in a "scrupulously honest" game. Having established that her lack of experience in carrying out such a mental task did not make her an efficient and speedy "bar lady," she had no fear that her delay in returning would arouse the suspicions of their intended victim.

Working swiftly and yet carefully, the "Duchess" arranged a deck of cards, identical to the one in use, so the hands would fall as they had on other occasions after a dupe had been primed and was ready for plucking. However, the task could not be performed until the seating arrangements around the table were settled, due to a mark being rendered less suspicious by being allowed to select whatever position he desired. The sequences she was setting out was such that, even if the victim elected to draw one card to replace the ace with the four jacks, the straight flush would still be made by Huckfield.

Having made everything ready, keeping a watch upon what was going on in the dining room through the partially open serving hatch, Emily poured the drinks for the "guests." Placing them on the tray she had used previously when supplying liquid refreshment, she held the prepared deck underneath it and timed her arrival to coincide with her husband completing the shuffling of the cards already in use.

Waiting until "Donna Maria" had cut the original deck, which would strengthen the belief that nothing untoward had taken place, the "Duchess" held out the loaded tray. After the "wealthy Brazilian" had accepted one of the glasses of wine, she served the Kid. Reaching with the haste that might be expected of one in a hurry to take a drink, he contrived to spill some of the liquor while accepting his glass. Growling an imprecation in his fluent Spanish, although of the kind spoken along the border between the United States and Mexico rather than in South America, he set the glass down untouched on the table. While the right hand began to rub at the front of his multicolored "trade" shirt, the left went into the outside pocket of the leather jacket as if in search of something with which to help dry its mate.

Giving "Manuel" no more than a cursory and slightly disgusted glance, Emily continued to distribute the drinks until reaching the "Duke"!

Waiting until the "Duchess" was extending the tray in the direction of her husband, holding it ready to exchange the two decks of cards, undetected in the manner she, he, and one of the "guests"—who handled the task when, as with Andrew Bullstrode, Emily was playing the "helpful sister" role—had perfected, the lady outlaw rose swiftly and threw the wine into her face.

Despite her claim to be a member of the French aristocracy, the profane exclamation that burst from the "Duchess" was in most *basic* English!

Emily's hands, rising instinctively to her eyes, which the liquid was stinging severely, released the tray and the cards sprayed in an incriminating cloud from beneath it!

Having been warned by Belle as to when and how the situation was likely to develop, the Kid had not been reaching for something with which to dry his right hand!

Instead, the disguised Texan had taken hold of the hollow wooden tube about six inches in length in the left-side pocket!

Seeing the time for inactivity was ended, much to his satisfaction, the Kid also came to his feet. Moving as he had spent much time in practicing since learning the part he was to play, he brought out the tube and raised it to his lips. At the same instant, he was sending his right hand beneath the near side of his jacket. As the other men around the table were showing consternation and starting to get up, he blew sharply into the tube. Propelled by the gust of air and moving faster than the human eye could follow, a sharp sliver of wood—its rearmost tip supplied with a piece of cotton wool dyed bright red for a flight—flew to bury its point in Chauvelin's left cheek.

Rising involuntarily, as his wife's had done, the fingers of the "Duke's" right hand touched the missile and he gave vent to a gasp of alarm!

Moving faster than any of the other "guests," Driberg sent his right hand toward the butt of his holstered revolver!

Spitting out a profanity seemingly at odds with his "cloth," Huckfield was the second swiftest to respond!

The other two "guests" were also reacting, but less rapidly due to carrying their handguns in positions that did not permit a speedy withdrawal. However, like their companions, they were devoting the majority of their attention to the only weapon—other than the "blowing pipe," which they realized would need to be recharged before it was available for further use— displayed by the "husband" of their intended victim. All were convinced the massive bowie knife also posed no threat to their well-being under the circumstances. Furthermore, the other two were taking comfort from remembering how competently the "cattle buyer" and the "preacher" had coped with hostile behavior on previous occasions.

To all the members of the gang who did not have other things on their minds, such as the leader and his wife, it seemed the discovery of the prepared deck was only a temporary setback. It would not, they felt sure, prevent the acquisition of the money brought by the beautiful "Brazilian." In fact, she would regret having made it so obvious she had detected the concealed cards for as long as she lived.

Which, the slowest pair of "guests" concluded, would only be for a short period more!

7

THERE IS A PRICE, NATURALLY

Despite being an acknowledged master in its use, the Ysabel Kid made no attempt to reach for and draw the massive, ivory-handled James Black bowie knife from its sheath!

Instead, the Texan's response was that of the *Pehnane* Comanche Dog Soldier he had been raised to be, combined with a frontier-trained gunfighter!

It was a most formidable combination!

Having appreciated there would be a need for a firearm and a means of carrying it in concealment more easily than would be possible with his enormous, four-pound, one-ounce, old Colt Second Model of 1848 Dragoon revolver, the Kid had had the problem solved for him. Returning with Belle Starr from escorting Andrew Bullstrode to the next town east along the railroad, he had found that Captain Dustine Edward Marsden "Dusty" Fog had reached Newton and was able to supply what was required.

Twisting the British-made Webley Irish Constabulary revolver he was already grasping from its spring-retention shoulder holster, the Texan cocked its hammer with his thumb regardless of the "double action" mechanism rendering this unnecessary. Turning it outward, he sent the first .450-caliber bullet into the left side of Thomas Driberg's chest before the Colt Peacemaker could be brought from leather and put to use.

Because Emily Chauvelin had contrived to pass on the fallacy supplied by the lady outlaw, "Reverend" Leslie Huckfield received a shock when he discovered the *"gaucho"* had a gun and was proving most competent with it. Nevertheless, although the shot that killed the "cattle buyer" was fired before he could collect the Remington Double Deringer from the outside right pocket of his black cutaway coat, he was not particularly alarmed. While carrying the weapon in such a fashion did not permit a really fast withdrawal, he had never found the need to adopt a means that did.

Three times in the past, when the need had arisen, the pose of being a member of the clergy had offered an element of surprise and Huckfield had not required any excessive speed. Therefore, he saw no reason for concern at present. He was confident that, having discounted him as a danger factor on account of his "religious" character "Manuel" would concentrate upon the other two "guests." This would allow him time to produce the twin-barreled pistol and open fire unimpeded.

On other occasions, the bogus preacher had succeeded because his deception was not discovered until it was too late for the victim to respond to the threat he posed!

Knowing Huckfield to be a member of the gang and—according to the information supplied by Belle—not the least dangerous of them, the Kid was not taken unawares. Thumbing back the hammer again while turning the short barrel of the Webley, he directed the second .450 bullet into the center of the gaunt man's forehead an instant before the Remington could be brought into alignment. Without speaking, as Huckfield was spinning around and following Driberg in falling lifeless to the floor, he swung the smoking weapon to encompass and cause the remaining pair of "guests" to freeze into immobility.

"Stand still, all of you!" Belle commanded, in echo to the second shot, still retaining the "Spanish" accent as an integral part of her scheme. Having dropped the glass as soon as she had thrown the wine, she had thrust her hand into the open mouth of her reticule. Bringing it out, grasping a small bottle filled with a thick, dark brown liquid, she pushed off the glass stopper with her thumb and went on, "This contains the only antidote for *curare* there is to be had *anywhere* in Kansas. Unless you do as I say, I will pour it on the floor and the 'Duke' will die in agony!"

The first words spoken by the lady outlaw were superfluous where the surviving pair of "guests" were concerned. No longer did the young man who was covering them appear in the least baby-faced or innocent. Rather, his dark features bore an expression of cold and relentless savagery that reminded them of paintings they had seen depicting Indians on the warpath. Crouching slightly behind the short-barreled revolver he had drawn so unexpectedly and already used with devastating effect upon two of their companions, he gave the impression of being ready, willing, and even eager to kill both of them if offered the slightest provocation.

Nor was the pose entirely simulated!

At such a moment, the Ysabel Kid—*Cuchilo*, "the

Knife," as he was known to his lodge brothers—
thought and reacted like a *Pehnane* Comanche brave-
heart warrior!

Which meant, where enemies were involved, the
Texan had little regard for the sanctity of human life!

Being just as alarmed by the transformation of
"Manuel," the attention of the "Duke" was not being
given to the smoking Webley revolver. Instead, he
was staring with horrified fascination from the sharp
spike he had plucked out of his cheek to the hollow
wooden tube also held by the Indian-dark young
"gaucho." There was a dark stain on the tip of the
former that, he concluded, was far too extensive to
have been caused by nothing more than blood from
the tiny wound it had inflicted. The tube was deco-
rated by symbols in red, white, blue, and green paint
such as he had seen upon Indian artifacts of various
kinds that had "medicine" significance.

Even as he was drawing his unpalatable and fright-
ening conclusions, Chauvelin heard a hiss of anger
from his wife. Turning his gaze toward her, he found
she was rubbing at her now reddened eyes and glaring
furiously at the cause of her misfortunes. Knowing
that her temper when roused was liable to produce
reactions not in keeping with her pose as being a
member of the French aristocracy, he guessed she was
on the point of rushing around the table and attacking
the beautiful "Brazilian" woman with tooth-and-nail
ferocity.

"Stay where you are, Emily!" the "Duke" howled
in alarm, realizing what the consequences of such a
hostile action was almost sure to be. "Do it, damn
you. That half-breed bastard shot me with this goddamned poisoned dart, and she'll throw the antidote
away if you go for her!"

"That I will, my dear 'Duchess,' " Belle supported,

starting to tilt the bottle slightly. "And you have my promise as one with the blood of a Spanish *grandee* on it!"

Regardless of having achieved the purpose for which the masquerade was intended, at least as far as obtaining proof of cheating, long experience warned the lady outlaw that she must keep to the character she had established. Having convinced the "Duke" and his gang that she and the Kid were the kind of people who could possess the lethal knowledge and means to use it, any suggestion of the truth would prevent them from reaching their desired goal.

As it was, everything depended upon Emily!

"Oh, my good god!" the "Duchess" shrieked, all her aggression departing along with the "French" accent, as she recollected the conversation about the deadly effect of such a device as was held by her husband. To give her credit, she loved him enough to care what might befall him as a result of the small wound it had inflicted. Swinging her now thoroughly frightened gaze to the lady outlaw, her tone took on a timbre of pleading as she resumed, "P—please give Armond the antidote!"

"Certainly," Belle answered. "But there is a price, naturally."

"T—take all the money on the table!" Emily offered hastily, and the "Duke" nodded an immediate concurrence.

"I was going to take that anyway," the lady outlaw claimed, gesturing toward the table with the bottle. "But I also want the twelve thousand, five hundred dollars you took from my *bueno amigo*, Andrew Bullstrode, a few nights ago."

"Do you know *him*?" the "Duchess" gasped.

"Very well indeed," Belle confirmed, and raised her left hand in a prohibitive fashion as Emily was about to speak. "No, do not try to pretend the innocent with me. Our families have done business together for many years and he told me what had happened when we met down the railroad track. That is why I brought 'Manuel' and sought you out, to get back all he lost to you. Now, make up your mind *muy pronto*, my dear 'Duchess.' The longer you delay, the less chance there is of your husband recovering from the effects of the poison."

"D—do as she says, Emily!" the "Duke" commanded, his face now gray with fear. He did not doubt for one moment, so convincingly had Belle acted, that a person of "Senora Donna Maria Constanza de la Santa Rosa's" kind would take such extreme measures to retrieve money out of which a business associate had been cheated. Being equally certain that the "Brazilian" beauty and her part-Indian "husband" were what they claimed and believing his life was in mortal peril, he went on, "Oh my god!"

"What is it?" the "Duchess" gasped.

"I—I feel d—dizzy!" Chauvelin croaked.

Waiting to hear no more, Emily dashed from the room.

8

WHAT WAS ON THAT SPIKE

"Well, I'll be switched!" the Ysabel Kid announced, returning the borrowed Webley Royal Irish Constabulary revolver to its shoulder holster on catching up with Belle Starr. He had been keeping the mansion under observation for a few minutes after they had taken their departure. "Dusty was *right*!"

"What about?" the lady outlaw inquired.

Having collected all the money from the table and received the loot belonging to General Jackson Baines "Ole Devil" Hardin and Andrew Bullstrode that the Chauvelins had had in another room, as Belle had suspected would be the case, she had ordered the "Duchess of Haute-Savoie" to accompany herself and "Manuel" to the front door. On crossing the threshold without interference by the other members of the gang, or giving any indication that she was not "Senora Donna Maria Constanza de la Santa Rosa," she had handed over the bottle of thick dark brown liquid. Then, as Emily had fled back to the dining room to administer the antidote without further delay, she had closed and locked the door. While the Kid, at his own suggestion, had remained in case there should be any attempt at pursuit, she had set off toward the business section of the town in which their hotel was situated. She had been confident that, should they be followed there later, the men who came would be deterred when learning the "Brazilian" beauty and her "husband" were in the company of Captain Dustine Edward Marsden "Dusty" Fog and other members of the OD Connected ranch's already legendary floating outfit.

"He reckoned when he loaned me this newfangled, itty-bitty stingy gun's how a man could *kill* somebody with it like it was my ole Dragoon thumb-buster and, seems like, you can at that,"[1] the Indian-dark young Texan explained. Then, putting aside his invariable pretense of having no faith in any kind of handgun except his massive, yet already obsolete revolver, he reported, "Anyways, there ain't *nobody* of 'em coming a-hunting after us for evens."

"That was your sneaky *Pehnane* Comanch' idea, I never thought there would be," the lady outlaw answered, gesturing with the reticule that was now bulging with the money acquired from the "Duke and Duchess of Haute-Savoie" and their reduced gang. "Not even for *this*."

"Well, blast it!" the Kid protested. "You didn't say's how I shouldn't need to keep watch!"

"Seeing how *eager* you were to do it, I didn't want to be so mean as to spoil your fun," Belle claimed with a smile. "After all, you men always know *best*."

_____

1. *An occasion when Captain Dustine Edward Marsden "Dusty" Fog, C.S.A., took advantage of the qualities of easy concealment offered by the British-made Webley Royal Irish Constabulary revolver and its shoulder holster is described in* Part One, "Small Man From Polveroso City, Texas," OLE DEVIL'S HANDS AND FEET *J.T.E.*

"I'd be the last to say 'no' to that," asserted the Texan. "Anyways, we pulled it off like you said we would, Belle!"

"You were so *convincing*," the lady outlaw praised. "Why, you almost had me believing you'd used a real 'blowing pipe' and poisoned dart, the way you looked, instead of a sharpened twig with red cotton wool to hold it in the tube and that boy's bean shooter I'd painted up so fancy. I know I wouldn't have wanted to come into the dark, hunting for somebody who was using a thing like that."

"Hell, I was close to forgetting who you are, way you acted all the time," the Kid responded, delighted by the compliment he had received. He had suspected, her acceptance of his support notwithstanding, she had had some doubts over whether he could play his part satisfactorily. Then a thought struck him and he went on, "Hey, though, that 'Duke' *hombre* allowed he was starting to feel dizzy and looked one real scared and sickened feller afore we left. Just what was on that spike you gave me?"

"Only some brown paint," Belle replied cheerfully. "His imagination and the way you backed my play did the rest. It hadn't affected him and couldn't beyond the slight sting when it hit, but I'm betting the antidote will."

"What was that brown stuff in the bottle?"

"Some croton oil, ipecac, cayenne pepper, and gunpowder, all mixed together like I was making a son-of-a-bitch stew. Once he gets that stuff working inside him, I'll bet he has to stay real *close* to the backhouse seat for a day or two."

"Whooee, and isn't that the living truth?" the Kid exclaimed, being aware the first two ingredients in particular had extremely potent laxative qualities even without having been—as range country cooks referred to a stew containing whatever items of food might be available—mixed until one did not know what each separate "son-of-a-bitch" might be. "I'd say he'll likely by wishing we had used a real poisoned dart and 'blowing pipe' on him afore he's through with it."

"Or it's through *him*," Belle supplemented. "I only wish I could have thought up some way to make dear Emily drink it as well. That would have taught her as well as the 'Duke' not to come wide-looping marks on my home range."

"You're a real mean woman, Miss Starr," the disguised Texan declared.

"I've never claimed I wasn't, Mr. Ysabel," the lady outlaw replied.

PART TWO

A FACE FROM THE PAST

9

I Need Your Help So Badly

"Excuse me, sir, please. But aren't you that most celebrated author and playwright Mr. David Icke?"

Although he was not using that name at the Railroad House Hotel in Mulrooney, Kansas, when he heard the attractive feminine voice that appeared to be charged with open admiration, the man to whom the question had been addressed turned to find out who was aware of his true identity. He was on his way to the reception desk to ask if there were any messages for him under the name he had given when registering, so he hoped the speaker—using his correct name—was not the person from whom he was expecting to hear.

Just over middle height, slender to the point of thinness, David Icke was in his late forties. He had lean, pallid, and, apparently, aesthetic features generally set in an expression indicative of a conscious superiority to those about him. Longish black hair dangled from beneath a rakish broad-brimmed black felt hat. Taken with the long black cloak lined with

red satin, brown pin-striped three-piece suit, white
silk shirt, flowing mauve cravat, and Hersome gaiter
boots, the headdress suggested he had a connection
with the arts or the theater. He showed no sign of
being armed in any fashion. Nor, to anybody conver-
sant with his advanced "liberal" point of view, would
he be expected to carry arms. He professed to have a
profound hatred of all firearms and had frequently
advocated, on suitable political platforms, that legisla-
tion preventing private ownership of them should be
ratified by Congress.

What Icke saw upon completing the turn, his
antipathy toward people with Southern accents—
especially those indicative of wealth and good
breeding—notwithstanding, made him feel pleased he
had been recognized. The only person close enough
to have spoken had drawn his attention in the dining
room of the hotel on more than one occasion, but she
had never, until now, given the slightest indication
that she knew who he was. She, on the other hand,
had been the frequent subject of his lecherous specula-
tions, even though he had considered these were
almost certain to remain unfulfilled.

The "celebrated author and playwright" had sought
to satisfy his curiosity with regards to the blonde, very
beautiful, curvaceous young woman standing before
him, despite feeling doubtful that anything was likely
to materialize from his knowledge. Her name, he had
discovered, was Darlene-Mae Abernathy and, as was
suggested by her always expensive attire and jewelry,
she was very wealthy. She had come from Richmond,
Virginia, to Mulrooney—accompanied, if rumor was
correct, by a dumpy and unprepossessing maid—
to attend to an important matter of business on behalf of her family. Whenever he had seen her, she
had always been in the company of Dennis Hobert; a
good-looking man of her own age who was employed

as a teller at the National Trust Bank in which Icke had deposited a large sum of money on arriving in the town.

Much to Icke's satisfaction, the beautiful young woman appeared to be alone at this moment!

"Why yes, Miss Abernathy," the "most celebrated author and playwright" confirmed, always willing to acknowledge his identity when it was requested in such a flattering manner. He did not pause to think it was surprising that a wealthy Southron would consider him in such a complimentary fashion, her kind being a major subject for vilification in his works. Instead, he noticed there was a reddening around her eyes as if she had recently been crying and other suggestions of some deeply disturbing emotion on her beautiful face. "That's who I am!"

"I hope you will forgive me for addressing you without our being formally introduced, s—!" the blonde began. "B-but how did you-all know my name?"

"I always try to learn the names of beatiful young ladies," Icke claimed, exuding an oily charm that he had found efficacious on numerous occasions in the past. "And, if I may say so, *you* are one of the most beautiful young ladies I've ever come across."

"I—I—don't f-feel very *beautiful* right now!" Darlene-Mae Abernathy complained, seeming on the verge of breaking into tears once more. "In fact, I feel so *miserable* I could just disgrace myself by starting to cry in public!"

"Surely not?" the playwright asked, and then continued, although his intentions were far less honorable than merely a desire to render assistance. "Is there *anything* I might be able to do for you?"

"Well, actually—er—that is why I sp—spoke to you," the blonde admitted, wringing her hands and showing suggestions of distress mingled with embarassment. "B-but it is no *use*. I just can't bring myself to talk out here in public!"

"Then we could go into the dining room," Icke suggested, hoping for a refusal on the same grounds.

"Th—That would be almost as public as out here!" Darlene-Mae pointed out.

"Then where would *you* feel comfortable for us to go and talk?" Icke inquired, believing the answer he was hoping for would prove more sutiable for his intentions if it came from the woman he was addressing.

"Well—!" the blonde said, hanging her head with an appearance of becoming modesty. "Unless you think it too *forward* of me, I—that is, although my maid isn't there to act as chaperone, perhaps you might be willing to come and talk in *my* room?"

"*Your* room?"

"I know it does sound *forward* of me, and I wouldn't think of making such an improper suggestion except—except—!"

"*Except?*" Icke prompted.

"Except—!" Darlene-Mae commenced hesitantly, then she finished in a rush. "I need *your* help so badly!"

"Then, my dear, I'm completely at your disposal!" the playwright stated, trying to look as if he was motivated by only the most honorable of intentions. "Shall we go to your room and you can tell me how I can be of service?"

Wondering what could be troubling the hitherto calm and poised Southern belle so deeply, but certain it was something far more serious than a ploy to make his acquaintance, Icke escorted her upstairs. Trying to decide how he could make the most of the opportunity with which he felt sure he was being presented, he forced himself to wait with what patience he could muster until she had led him into her second-floor front room. Even then, he concluded it would be advisable to allow her to make the first move.

"I—I—!" the blonde began, having seated her guest at the writing table. "I hardly know where to begin, nor *how*, if ind—!"

"Start at the beginning," the playwright suggested.

"I-it's my half brother, Dennis—!" Darlene-Mae started to oblige.

"Dennis?" Icke inquired, despite feeling sure he could supply the answer himself.

"Dennis Hobert. You've seen him at the National Trust Bank, I believe. And you may have seen him in the hotel here with me."

"I remember him. He's a teller at the bank, isn't he?"

"Y-yes. But he's also in such *trouble*—!"

"What kind of trouble?" Icke inquired, with an interest that was suddenly genuine.

Having a secret and vastly more lucrative business than that of author, playwright, and radical political speaker, the dapperly dressed man had on more than one occasion found banks tellers in trouble to be—if nothing more—a useful source of information.

"S-*serious* tr—trouble," the blonde replied, if far from succinctly. "H-he—W-well, since coming west, he's fallen in with such *bad* company and—and—!"

"And?"

"Well, he's been g-gam—*gambling*!"

"Gambling?"

"Heavily!"

"And losing heavily, too!" Icke guessed, deciding he was hearing an all-too-familiar story and wondering how he was supposed to help in it unless he was to be subjected to a request for a "loan" to repay the losses.

"And I—losing *far* more than he could afford," the beautiful blonde confirmed, twisting a tiny handkerchief between her hands and showing distress over having to make such a confession.

"And now he's in debt?"

"N-not in the way you think!"

"Then in what way is he in debt?"

"The m-men he owed the money to are *dangerous* brutes. Poor Dennis had to pay them what was owing or—or—or they—!"

"They'd have hurt him," Icke supplied, still uncertain whether the blonde was genuine or merely trying to persuade him to part with money by playing upon his sympathy. If the latter was the case, anybody who knew him could have warned her the effort was wasted. While he advocated sharing the wealth of others with those less fortunate than themselves, like most of his kind, his charity began and remained strictly at home. "So, as he didn't show signs of being hurt when I last saw him, I presume he must have paid what he owed to them?"

"He did!"

"May I ask *how* he paid?"

"B-by borrowing m-money—!"

"*Borrowing* money?"

"F-from the bank!"

"*Borrowing* money from the *bank*?" Icke challenged, having found repetition a useful way of winning confidences from hesitant or reluctant sources such as the blonde.

"Th—That's how he g—came by it," Darlene-Mae claimed, but far too defensively to make the affair sound as innocent as she wanted it to.

"Let me get this straight," Icke requested and, although feeling sure such was *not* the case, he went on, "You mean he went to Mr. Cockburn, the owner of the bank, and *asked* for a loan?"

"If only he *had*!" the blonde wailed, shuffling her feet in embarrassment. "H-he took it without anybody else's knowledge, confident he could repay it long before it was missed—!"

"And now he can't?" Icke stated, instead of asked, having heard variations of the story in the past and having no doubt that he could turn it to his advantage as was the case on those previous occasions.

"N-not nearly as quickly as has become necessary!"

"I'm sorry, but I don't follow you!"

"Our family would willingly have made good the loss, even though the sum is almost twenty thousand dollars, to save our good name. But—!"

"But?"

"Unfortunately," Darlene-Mae explained, with the air of having come to the crux of the matter. "The Federal bank examiners are arriving tomorrow and—!"

"Hell's fires!" Icke exclaimed, coming to his feet hurriedly.

"Is something *wrong*?" Darlene-Mae inquired, showing alarm at the change that had come over her visitor.

"Wrong?" Icke snarled, the words erupting from his mouth as he glared savagely at the beautiful yet clearly perturbed young woman. Then, when he saw the consternation his behavior seemed to be arousing, he made a visible effort to regain control over his churned-up emotions. After a moment, except for his eyes, he contrived to remove the glowering from his features. Taking a gold watch from the pocket of his vest, he flicked open its cover and checked the time. With a sensation of relief, he concluded that he could reach the National Trust Bank before it was closed for the day. He also considered there might be a way through which he could capitalize upon the situation where Darlene-Mae was concerned. Forcing his voice to take on a less aggressive timbre, he went on soothingly, "No, my dear. There's nothing *wrong*. I—I felt a cramp in my leg and stood up."

"Is it all right?" the blonde asked, her manner suggesting solicitude.

"Yes, it's going off now," Icke replied, having started to rub at his left leg to lend confirmation to his excuse. "You know, my dear, I've been thinking. There's a way I might be able to help your half brother."

"How, sir?" Darlene-Mae asked, taking on an appearance of aroused hope mingled with possible gratitude.

"I'm not without influence in Mulrooney, you know," Icke commenced, then realized there was something that might tend to detract from the declaration and lessen the effect he was seeking to create. "Of course, as you undoubtedly know, I'm staying here at the hotel under an assumed name. I have to do it, you understand, to avoid unwanted attentions being directed my way."

"Why, I can just *imagine* that a gentleman of your great talent would have to do nothing else," the blonde asserted. "In fact, 'though I recognized you-all straightaway and wanted to do so from the start, that is why I didn't make myself known to you before this afternoon."

"And I'd have been *delighted* to make an exception in your case, if you had made yourself known earlier," Icke stated, barely restraining an impulse to reach for the blonde's hand, as he realized that to do so prematurely could spoil his ambitions where she was concerned. Replacing his watch and adjusting the hang of its chain across his vest, he continued, "Anyway, I think the best thing I can do is go to the bank and intercede on behalf of your half brother."

"Intercede?"

"Banker Cockburn and I are old friends and I'm sure he will listen to what I have to say, then act upon it."

"Well, heavens to Betsy, would you just *credit*

that?" Darlene-Mae gasped. Then she adopted an attitude that would have won over a man with far more honorable designs upon her than those of her visitor. "But why would you do that for Dennis?"

"While it will help *him*, it's really *you* I'm doing it for," Icke corrected, wanting to avoid leaving any doubt over the direction in which his efforts were intended. "Of course, I would try to help any young man in difficulty. But I count it a special honor and privilege to be of service to *you*."

"My, and they say Yankees aren't gallant!" the blonde purred. "You won't find me *ungrateful* for anything you can do, sir."

"Then why don't you call me 'David'?"

"May I?"

"I wish you would," Icke declared, deciding he was achieving his purpose.

"Then, *David*, you must call me, 'Darlene-Mae,' " the blonde authorized, and glanced pointedly at the clock on the wall. "Great heavens, is *that* the time?"

"It is," Icke confirmed, having had his thoughts jerked from lechery to the more vitally important matter under discussion. On the point of crossing to the door, he was struck by a thought. "Will your half brother be there when I arrive?"

"No," Darlene-Mae replied. "I told him that he should send word to Banker Cockburn that he was suffering from the grippe and must stay away today. I was afraid that he might say or do something which could betray himself, if he was to go there under the *strain* he was suffering. Was I *wrong* to give him such advice?"

"Of course you weren't *wrong*, my dear!" Icke confirmed, being aware of how easily a man normally honest could betray himself after having behaved in such an illicit fashion. He was genuinely sincere as he went on, "As a matter of fact, you gave him just the advice I would have, if I had known about it earlier. Well, time's flying and I'd better be getting along."

"You will let me know how you get on, won't you, David?" the blonde requested, looking so pathetically eager she might have softened the heart of a confirmed misogynist and the man she was addressing was far from that. "If you come straight back to me on your return, unless you think this too *forward* of me, I will have a bottle of brandy waiting to toast your success and our continued *friendship*."

"I'll do just that," Icke promised, and despite his anxiety over realizing that he had allowed more time to slip by than he intended before taking his departure, he felt sure that coming back with the "news" he would deliver was going to prove worthwhile.

"Goodbye for now, David. May you soon return," Darlene-Mae purred. "And the very *best* of luck!"

10

YOU DON'T BELIEVE HE IS?

Telling himself the "very *best* of luck" he could have had under the circumstances was to have met Darlene-Mae Abernathy and learned in time of the trouble that was coming to the National Trust Bank, in which he had deposited a large sum of money for sakekeeping, David Icke wasted no time on leaving her room. Having no need to go to his own quarters, farther along the passage, he hurried downstairs. Crossing the reception lobby, for once he was relieved by receiving a negative shake of the head from the clerk at the desk. The last thing he required at that moment was to be informed that the message he was expecting had arrived. It was imperative that nothing further delay him before he set out to retrieve the fifteen thousand dollars, not even the arrival of the criminals for whom it was intended.

There had been a very good reason for the agitation Icke had displayed on being informed by the blonde of her half brother's peculations at the bank!

Although having acquired a certain fame as an

author, a playwright and a politician of radical views, Icke was only moderately successful at any of them. Certainly he did not maintain his far-from-meager standard of living on his earnings from all three sources. His main income was acquired by having invested money accrued some years earlier by less-than-legal means and becoming, in complete secrecy, one of the major receivers of stolen property anywhere in the United States of America. He was, in fact, the biggest "fence" on the Atlantic seaboard.

Having had a proposal reach him to purchase a quantity of very valuable jewelry, looted farther west from a hunting party of European aristocrats, Icke had put aside his reluctance to travel beyond the Mississippi River and come to Mulrooney. One of the stipulations of the deal was that he must be prepared to hand over the fifteen thousand dollars, quoted as the price for the illicit merchandise, in cash when it was delivered to him. He had been warned that, should the sum not be immediately forthcoming, the loot would be taken elsewhere. As the stolen property was worth far more and, in fact, could be returned to its owners at a very good profit, without any questions being asked, he had known it would present no problems for the thieves to find another fence ready, willing and eager to negotiate. They would not hesitate before going to semebody else.

Considering it could prove the most lucrative single deal in which he had ever participated, Icke had done as instructed. Because of wishing to avoid arousing suspicions with regard to possessing finances far beyond anything produced through his literary and political activities, he kept only a small bank account in his own name. However, having had no desire to leave a trail that might be traced back to him, he had been unwilling to make use of one of the accounts he maintained under various aliases. Therefore, he had brought the money with him. It had not come from any of his accounts, but was in bills he had acquired following a robbery in New York, bills that were still too "hot" to be passed through any legitimate outlet. Nevertheless, provided they were unaware of this—which he considered likely to be the case—he was hoping they would be accepted by the unsuspecting Western outlaws.

Always wary, Icke was disinclined to keep such a large sum of even "clean" money upon his person, hidden in his room, or leave it in the safe of the manager of the Railroad House Hotel. To avoid relying upon any of these methods, he had secreted the fifteen thousand dollars in a safety deposit box at the National Trust Bank. As yet, there had not been any word from the outlaws and he had seen no need to withdraw it.

The situation, the receiver realized, had changed with dramatic suddenness due to the information he had received!

Once the Federal bank examiners found the deficit created by Dennis Hobert's peculations, Icke was certain he would not be able to retrieve his property from the safety-deposit box until the matter had been settled. Nor was this the worst of the situation. Should the investigations of the examiners require it, they were empowered to open and check the contents of the safety-deposit boxes. If this happened, it was possible the true source of the money he had left would be discovered. He was all too aware of the consequences for him to regard the contingency with equanimity.

Yet another matter had caused perturbation to Icke as he heard the news. Past experience had taught him that criminals, who rarely trusted any fence too far, were disinclined to wait for payment to be forthcoming. In fact, he had already been warned by the

present gang that such would prove the case. Therefore, he had been alarmed by the thought that the
peculations of the teller could be endangering the
most potentially lucrative negotiations of their kind in
which he had ever been engaged.

On leaving the hotel, the receiver found himself wishing the two bodyguards he had hired were
with him!

Being disinclined to trust the outlaws from whom
he was expecting to purchase the jewelry, the receiver
had had a contact in Kansas engage Stephen Forey and
Lee Potter as bodyguards. However, he had found
reason to require their assistance even sooner than
anticipated. Discovering that he was being followed by
a young man with reasons to hate him bitterly, he had
decided to take precautions. The trap he had laid did
not produce the required results. Despite the failure of
the two hard cases to kill Geoffrey Crayne, which they
had attributed to a large and very aggressive Irish-
woman having mistaken their proposed victim for
somebody with whom she had a close acquaintance,
he had not disposed of their services. Being in an unfa-
miliar region, his previous period west of the Mississippi River having been confined to Oklahoma, he had
no personal knowledge of where he might be able to
procure replacements. Nor did he wish to be without
some form of protection.

Having guessed why Crayne was following him,
wearing a disguise, Icke had believed there would
continue to be a threat to his life from that source
and, if possible, wanted to have it removed before
returning to his usual stamping grounds. While the
termination could be arranged in the East, he considered it advisable to happen in Mulrooney without,
ostensibly, it having any connection with him. However, although there had been no trace of the young
Bostonian since the abortive attempt, he was disin-

clined to take the chance that the quest for vengeance was called off due to the other being frightened from Mulrooney by the narrow escape he had had. He felt sure Crayne would not give up so easily.

Notwithstanding the desire for protection against the young Bostonian and, perhaps, the outlaws with whom he would be dealing, the parsimonious nature of the receiver would not cover the cost of having his bodyguard take rooms at the hotel he was using. Instead, they were staying and paying for their own accommodation elsewhere, reporting to him for orders every morning. Having had neither the reason nor the inclination to go out that day, regardless of how he had been dressed on coming from his room, he had told them to continue their search for Crayne when he last saw them. He had no idea where they might now be looking, so he was unable to send a message demanding their attendance.

Now, due to the unanticipated turn of events that he had been fortunate enough to discover, Icke was wishing he had the pair readily available to act as escort until he had retrieved his money and secured it in the safe at the hotel. However, he took what comfort he could from the thought that the bank was only a short distance away from his temporary accommodation and both were in an area far more adequately protected by the local peace officers than the district with the shipping pens for cattle into which he had lured Crayne two days earlier.

Hurrying to the bank, the receiver was alert for any sign that the secret of the peculations by Hobert had become public knowledge. With relief, he saw nothing to suggest this might be the case. Certainly there was no crowd of worried depositors outside, either waiting patiently or clamoring to withdraw savings before it was too late to save them from being impounded.

On entering the building, Icke found it was devoid of clients and on the point of being closed. The only employees present were one of the guards, standing by the main entrance, and a solitary teller, who was no longer young, behind the counter. Nevertheless, although the actual conversation was inaudible, voices could be heard from beyond the door inscribed "CYRUS B. COCKBURN, Private."

Suspecting the books were being inspected, prior to the forthcoming visit by the Federal bank examiners, the receiver decided there was still an urgent need to regain possession of his money. Being a man of integrity, Cockburn would consider it his duty on discovering the deficit caused by Hobert to withold all the assets pending an official investigation. There was no telling how long this state of affairs might continue. Nor did Icke wish to go through the formalities required to bring a similar sum from one of his bank accounts in the East, despite having more than sufficient resources to do so. For one thing, this would cause him to pay with honest rather than "hot" money and still leave the problem of disposing of the latter.

Crossing to the counter, Icke thought he detected a somewhat strained air about the solitary, gray-haired and parchment-faced teller and wondered whether he might, in fact, have arrived too late. With some trepidation, he explained the reason for his visit. Anxiety bit at him as the edlerly man he was addressing directed a look toward the guard at the front door. However, after having next glanced in a surly and disgruntled fashion at the clock on the wall, the teller picked up a small bunch of keys and came through the gateway giving access to the customer's section.

"Are you all on your own today?" Icke inquired, accompanying the still-scowling old man to collect his property from the safety-deposit box he had rented, which was kept with the others in the well-protected basement of the building.

"Yes!" the teller answered shortly, concentrating upon selecting and manipulating the keys necessary to gain admission to the vault.

"Where's the young man I saw when I took the box?"

"He sent word this morning that he's gone down with the grippe!"

"And you don't believe he has?"

"It isn't for *me* to say whether he has or hasn't!" the teller stated, having been reproved by Cockburn for making such a suggestion when the message from Hobert had arrived. It had done nothing to decrease his animosity toward his younger and more forceful colleague; nor had having been required to deal with the extra work caused by the absence. "But his *grippe* came on very suddenly, if you ask me!"

Satisfied that the peculations had not yet come to light, Icke decided against continuing the conversation. He had no desire for his interest in Hobert to be mentioned to the Federal bank examiners. If this should happen, it might cause them to want to check upon the leather dispatch case he had come to collect. Therefore, he lapsed into silence and his informant showed no signs of wishing to continue speaking. Instead, each used the key he had brought to unlock and open the safety-deposit box.

Taking out the case, although the box no longer held any of his property, the receiver announced he would continue the rental. Seeing nothing out of the ordinary about the instructions and being interested only in finishing work for the day, the teller raised no objections to his pocketing the key. Returning to the ground floor and passing the guard, who was waiting with obvious impatience to close and lock the door, he left the bank satisfied he had been in time to avoid having his money impounded along with the rest of its assets and holdings.

Hurrying to the hotel, Icke felt his anxieties ebbing away and being replaced by a sensation of elation. He was sure that, on hearing the story he was concocting, the beautiful blonde would be putty in his hands as soon as she heard that the visit—supposedly to extract her brother from difficulty—had been "successful." Nevertheless, in the event that gratitude and a judicious plying with the brandy she had promised to acquire did not prove sufficient to render her compliant, he was convinced that the presentation of a marijuana cigarette—from the case he always carried— would induce a condition wherein she would become sexually forthcoming. Such tactics had failed him only once, but he had contrived to avoid suffering the consequences of his narcotic-induced attack upon the sister of Geoffrey Crayne. He promised himself that, being in an area where he could exert less influence, he would ensure nothing of a similar nature occurred on this occasion.

11

MAY WE BOTH GET WHAT WE WANT

Entering the Railroad House Hotel, David Icke was not allowed to follow the line of action he had planned. It was his intention to make arrangements with the recepion clerk at the desk to have the leather dispatch case put in the safe, before going upstairs to carry out the seduction he believed would soon be his for the asking. However, as he came through the front entrance, he saw Darlene-Mae Abernathy walking down from the second floor.

"Hello, Dav—'Mr. Wilson'!" the blonde greeted, hurrying toward the receiver. "I saw you coming from the bank and I just couldn't wait any longer. So I came down to meet you. Were you *successful* with—with—?"

"With my *negotiations*?" Icke suggested.

"With your *negotiations*?" Darlene-Mae accepted.

"Completely *successful*," the receiver replied, truthfully as far as it went. That, however, was the end to his veracity. "Don't worry, Darl—*Miss Abernathy*. Everything is settled and, providing your family are willing to make good the money, your half brother has nothing to fear."

"Well, thank *heavens* for that!" the blonde declared, coming forward to take Icke by the left arm. "Or, rather, thank *you*, David!"

"It was nothing," the receiver claimed, once again with truth.

"But it means so *much* to dear Dennis!" Darlene-Mae gasped, squeezing at the arm she was holding. "Why—I could just give you a great big hug and kiss!"

"Here?" Icke asked, glancing around the reception lobby.

"Oh heavens to Betsy, what you must think of me!" the beautiful blonde gasped, looking around her with such innocent alarm it seemed butter would have a hard time melting in her mouth. Nevertheless, retaining her grip on his arm, she continued, "Come, let's go upstairs first."

"First?" the receiver queried.

"I promised that I would have a bottle of brandy waiting in my room so we could toast your success with Banker Cockburn," Darlene-Mae explained. "Or had you forgotten about it?"

"No, of course I hadn't forgotten," Icke stated, but dropped his gaze to the case in his right hand. "But I meant t—!"

"Don't you want to come with me?" the blonde demanded, a touch of petulance coming into her voice.

"I most certainly do want to come—!" the receiver confirmed, but was not allowed to say anything more.

"Then let's go and do it straightaway!" Darlene-Mae ordered rather than merely requested, her manner that of a person long accustomed to having every whim fulfilled immediately and who was likely to go into a fit of sulks, if nothing worse, should she not get her own way.

"Whatever you say, my dear," Icke assented, being unwilling to forfeit the opportunity he was confident he had created, and struggling to control his resentment. Then he told himself that, as the money would not be out of his sight until it could be put into the safe, he need not feel concerned over it. "Come on, then. Let's go up to your room and drink to my success and your half brother's salvation."

On the way to the second floor, possessing a suspicious and untrusting nature, the receiver started to worry over the insistence of the blonde in going to her room. The feeling was intensified when she asked about the dispatch case. However, on being told it contained documents concerning the business he had carried out with Banker Cockburn as a prelude to rescuing her half brother, her attitude implied she was not really interested and had merely been making conversation.

Allowing Icke to precede her into her room, Darlene-Mae closed and locked the door. Before he could register any concern over the actions, she turned and smiled with a mixture of demure provocation that drove the suspicion from his head. Removing and draping his cloak over a chair, he forgot his earlier misgivings and contemplated only the benefits he anticipated would soon be coming his way.

"Have a seat, David," the blonde offered.

"Will *here* be all right?" the receiver hinted, crossing to sit on the bed with the case by his side.

"Wherever you wish," Darlene-Mae assented, going to the dressing table. "I had the brandy brought up while you were away, being so *sure* you would be successful. I trust what they brought is a satisfactory *vintage*— Is that what it is called?"

"One doesn't usually refer to the vintage of a *brandy*," Icke corrected, looking at the bottle for which the blonde was reaching. Neither it nor the tray and two glasses had been on the dressing table when he had left to visit the bank. "But it's the best brand they have in the hotel."

"I'm pleased to hear that," the blonde claimed. "I know so little about such things, and I do so want us to have the best."

"You got it there," the receiver assured, watching the bottle being uncorked by his hostess. "But wasn't there something said about me getting a hug and a kiss for saving your half brother?"

"Why, there most certainly *was*," Darlene-Mae affirmed. "Although it seems such a *small* price to pay for having poor Dennis's good name saved from being besmirched. I'm sure my family would feel you deserve a far better reward than just a hug and a kiss from li'l ole me."

"What better reward could anybody ask than that?" Icke asked.

"But it's so *little!*" the blonde protested. "I know a *gentleman* like you would be offended if I was to offer you *money* on behalf of Dennis and the rest of the family, but perhaps we can think of *something* else?"

While carrying out the conversation, Darlene-Mae had opened the bottle. Pouring out two liberal quantities, she set it back on the tray and took up the two glasses. If her guest had been watching closely, he still might have failed to detect the small white tablet—which she had been palming as deftly as a magician specializing in sleight of hand—being slipped into the drink on the left. Moving both glasses in a rotating motion, apparently trying to duplicate how she had seen it done when serving such a liquor, she speeded the process of dissolving.

"Not that it matters, and I certainly didn't help your half brother with any idea of being *rewarded*," Icke said, trying to sound sincere in the declaration. "But what else did you have in mind?"

"Heavens to Betsy, I've no *idea*," the blonde replied, eyeing the receiver coyly and yet also conveying an impression that she had given thought to the form of reimbursement. "I've never before been involved in any such a thing. However, shall we drink our toast first?" She paused, but did not allow time for anything to be said by her guest. "My old daddy always used to claim a drink made a *kiss* so much more enjoyable."

"Then who are we to argue with the wisdom of your daddy?" Icke inquired cheerfully, feeling even more certain that the seduction he was planning would be a sinecure. Accepting the left-hand glass, but seeing not the slightest trace of the addition to its contents, he went on, "Do you want to propose the toast, or shall I?"

"Why not you first, then I'll propose one in return?" Darlene-Mae suggested.

"Ladies first, I always say," the receiver countered.

"Very well," the blonde agreed. "There was something else my old daddy used to say, though for the life of me I can't *imagine* what he meant. He always claimed that, if you wanted to know what kind of *lover* a man is, watch him drink and, should he drain off his glass straightaway, you'll know he's a good one."

"That sounds excellent advice to me," Icke declared, suspecting the beautiful Southron was less innocent and naive than she seemed. However, the supposition did not cause him any concern at that moment. It merely led him to believe his plans for the immediate future, as she appeared to be compliant and even eager to provoke what he had in mind, would be so much easier. "And we should drink to it!"

"So we will, *eventually*," Darlene-Mae promised, raising her glass. "First, however, let's drink to the success you had at the bank and may we both get what we want."

"I'm all for the last!" the receiver asserted eagerly. Wanting to impress the blonde, he raised and drained his glass. Coughing a little, he noticed something that caused him to say, "Aren't you drinking?"

"I'll finish it in a moment," Darlene-Mae answered, having merely wet her lips on the glass of brandy she was holding. Placing it on the tray from which it had come, she reached up to start unfastening the neck of the white silk blouse she wore. "But I feel just a little warm and thought, providing you don't *object*, of course, I would make myself a little more *comfortable* first."

"Now, why should I *object* to th—!" Icke commenced, then frowned and stared as if at something that was moving. Blinking his eyes, which were becoming glazed, he tried and failed to stop the glass from slipping from his fingers. A look of dull alarm mingled with puzzlement came to his face, and trying to shove himself erect, he continued, "Wha—Wha—Whash—Whash—hap—happen—?"

Before the question could be completed, the receiver crumpled backward to lie half on and half off the bed, breathing stertorously.

"You've been drugged is what's happened, you Yankee son of a bitch!" the beautiful blonde explained, her face and voice as coldly implacable as that of a judge sentencing a criminal to a death that was well-deserved. "But that's only the *start* of your troubles!"

12

I'VE GOT TO YOU TOO LATE

For several seconds after consciousness returned, David Icke felt as if he was being twirled around and up and down rapidly. Having forced apart lids reluctant to obey the dictates of his mind, he closed his eyes quickly to block off the dazzling effect of a bright light from somewhere in the center of the whirling vortex above him. Then the sensation of dizziness began to ebb away. As this happened, he found his faculties were starting to function. Apart from a slightly unpleasant taste in the mouth and a temporary lapse of memory, the comment made by Darlene-Mae Abernathy after he had passed out notwithstanding, the potion added without his knowledge to his brandy was producing no serious aftereffects.

With the settling down of his emotions, a careful peek and a few seconds of thought informed the receiver that he was lying on a bed in a room much like the one he had rented at the Railroad House Hotel in Mulrooney, Kansas. It was much tidier than he kept his own, however. The previous discomfort to his optic nerves, he discovered, had resulted from nothing more than a somewhat anemic lamp suspended from the ceiling.

Slowly a recollection of the events that had occurred immediately prior to his collapse on the bed began to force itself upon Icke!

Snarling a profanity, the receiver thrust himself into a sitting position and gazed wildly about him!

The beautiful blond Southron, upon whose virtue—assuming it was still intact and unsullied—Icke had had licentious designs, was nowhere to be seen!

Nor, a glance followed by a more careful scrutiny informed the receiver, was the leather dispatch case—containing the fifteen thousand dollars' purchase price for the jewelry he had been offered—on the bed where he had placed it!

There was even worse to come!

Having risen from the bed, meaning to commence what he suspected was going to prove a vain attempt to find the case lying on the floor, Icke noticed in passing his reflection in the mirror on the dressing table. Continuing to glare elsewhere, something he had noticed caused him to return his gaze to it. For a moment, apart from the not unexpected expression of shock and alarm on his pallid—now ashy—features, he could discern nothing to suggest what had partially attracted his attention.

Then the receiver realized something definitely was not as it should be!

A close look informed Icke there was no longer a gold chain suspended between the pockets of his vest. Grabbing fingers quickly ascertained that it and the watch to which it was attached had both gone. Goaded by the consternation that the discovery was causing, his hands scrabbled hastily at the inside pockets of his jacket. It was as he had feared. His well-filled wallet had also been taken by the blonde; but something far, *far*, more important was missing.

Aware that his illicit occupation might be exposed to the authorities one day, creating a need for immediate flight, Icke always took certain precautions against that eventuality. One of these was to keep in his possession at all times a red morroco leather pocketbook containing the relevant details concerning all his secret bank accounts. Discovering that it too had been taken by Darlene-Mae Abernathy was an even more shattering blow than the loss of the case he had retrieved from the National Trust Bank, his gold watch and chain and the wallet containing all his ready money, except for the change in his trousers pockets.

While the details of where the accounts were deposited, the aliases employed, and all the other necessary information were written in a code of his own devising, the receiver realized this was far from an inviolable system of protection. Regardless of possessing a high opinion of his own intelligence, he was willing—under the current deeply disturbing circumstances—to admit someone else might be sufficiently astute to decipher what he had written. Furthermore, he could not recollect enough of the details to enable him to make contact with the various banks and give orders to prevent withdrawals until he was in a position to transfer the money elsewhere. To make matters much worse, even at his home, he did not have any other record to supply the requisite information.

On the point of dashing out to send for Stephen Forey and Lee Potter to come and join him, a thought struck Icke. Telling himself he was merely wasting his time, but in a frame of mind eager to grasp at straws no matter how unproductive they were likely to be, he started to search the room to see if he could find some clue to help locate the beautiful blonde. Apart from a woman's long and hooded black cloak hanging upon a peg in the big wardrobe, there was nothing left to prove she had even been in occupation. The clock on the wall informed him it was seven forty-five, and although the drapes were drawn, various noises coming through the partially open window implied this was evening and not morning.

Donning his cloak and leaving the room, no better informed about the woman calling herself "Darlene-Mae Abernathy" than when he had entered—except for believing this was unlikely to be her name and knowing she had tricked him—the receiver hurried down to the ground floor. Crossing the reception lobby, he was about to ask for a bellboy to deliver a message summoning his bodyguards when he saw the clerk gazing past him with a pained expression. Hearing the name by which he was registered spoken from his rear, in a slightly guttural accent such as he had become accustomed to during the period of his life spent in Oklahoma, he turned. Coming toward him was a tall, lean, and Indian-dark man dressed and armed after the fashion of the cowhands he had seen around Mulrooney.

"Are you speaking to me?" Icke asked, always wary when in contact with anybody who sounded like a native of Oklahoma and alert for any suggestion that he had been recognized from the time he spent there.

"I'm not meaning that lard-gutted *hombre* back of the bar there, looking like he's all scared I'm going to start wide-looping the spitoons," the newcomer answered, directing a sardonic nod at the desk clerk. "And, 'less there's *two* looks and dresses fancy, you're that same 'Mr. Wilson' as I've seen around town with Stevie Forey and Lee Potter. But, happen you ain't him, say no 'n' I'll quit wasting my time."

"I'm the same," the receiver confirmed, unable to

detect any suggestion of recognition from the past and hoping he was not being addressed by a member of the gang who had offered to sell him the stolen jewelry. He could not think of any other reason for the visit. "What can I do for you?"

"I reckon's how that'd be something you'd rather listen to where there ain't no ears a-wagging 'n' a-flapping to take it all in," the Oklahoman stated, his dark features being indicative of Indian blood, once again favoring the man behind the reception desk with a nod. "Like over in that fancy barroom, was I asked."

"Come with me," Icke ordered, and leading the way, selected a table clear of the other occupants. Sitting down and waving away the waiter who started to approach, he went on, "Well, what is it?"

"I reckon I've got to you too late," the Oklahoman asserted, studying the haggard face of his obviously reluctant host.

"To late for *what*?"

"To warn you about 'Gold-Brick Annie O'Toole' and her sister."

"Who the hell are they?"

"You likely never looked twice at Winnie O'Toole, her being what I'd call's homely as a mud fence. But the 'Gold-Brick's' that real purty blond-haired gal's been living here calling herself 'Darlene-Mae Abernathy.' "

"Why do you call her 'Gold-Brick'?" Icke demanded, although he could guess.

"It's 'cause she goes 'round selling gold bricks from her daddy's mine, only it comes out he's mining lead with gold paint on it; or other things that ain't what they look like, to fellers's don't have enough sense to pack sand into a rathole. She's what I've heard tell's called a 'conjuneero.' "

"A goddamned confidence trickster!" the receiver spat out, despite never having heard such a term for a criminal following that particular vocation.

"Between 'em, the 'Gold-Brick' 'n' her sister are about the best around," confirmed the Oklahoman. "I knowed they must be on the trail of some poor son of a bitch when I saw 'em all fancied up like a rich gal and her maid. So they took *you* down, huh?"

"Took me *down*?" Icke growled, trying to behave as if he could not comprehend the meaning of the question.

"I know you big city jaspers don't spend a whole heap of time out in the sun," the Indian-dark visitor elaborated dryly. "But your face's whiter'n a dead fish's belly 'n' you look some sicker'n a deacon's's drunk Taos Lightning 'stead of holy water. Yes sir, mister. They took you down and likely left you drugged. I should've figured's how they'd got set to bring down whoever they was after when I saw them having their gear moved out this afternoon."

"This afternoon?"

"Right after you'd come out and was hightailing it to the bank."

"Then why didn't you stop them?"

"The last feller's got took with such a notion didn't tote it no further'n to get put under a li'l wooden cross in boothill, mister. Which I wasn't figuring on taking the chance on joining him when I didn't know's I'd get paid should I pull it off."

"So they've left town, have they?" Icke snarled, deciding the dark-faced and dangerous-looking man had something more in mind than merely supplying the information given up to that point.

"I said they'd lit a shuck out of this here fancy rooming house, was all," corrected the Oklahoman.

"You mean they're still in Mulrooney?"

"I mean nothing else but they're still here in Mulrooney."

"And you can tell me whereabouts?"

"Now, isn't that the goddamned strangest thing?" the Oklahoman drawled, leaning back in his chair, his face taking on a crafty expression. "I could've swored's how I knowed where they was, when I come in here. But, dog-my-cats, if it hasn't gone plumb out of my mind!"

"Would five dollars help you remember?" Icke asked, having that much in coins left in the pockets of his trousers.

"Mister," the visitor answered, straightening up with an expression of disdain. "If that's all you reckon what they've took you for is worth—!"

"I've got some money in my room," the receiver said bitterly, although the currency to which he was referring was more readily available even than that. Another of his precautions against the need for a hurried departure was always to keep a one-hundred-dollar bill in the hollow built into each heel of whichever shoes or boots he was currently wearing. "But I'm not going to hand any of it over until I'm sure you're not just trying to put something over on me."

"You don't put much trust in other folks, do you?"

"I'm not a sucker, if that's what you mean. And, if it comes down to a point, I don't know anything about you. Not even your name."

"They do tell even my own pappy never knowed *that*," the Oklahoman drawled. "Which being, you wouldn't know whether I'd spoke truthful or just given you a summer name. Anyways, this I'll give you for starters, mister. They're hiding out in a shack I can show you down to the poor folks' end of town. At least, Winnie's there. The 'Gold-Brick's' gone off with some good-looking young feller and, happen I've heard right about her hot-assed ways, she won't be back for a fair spell."

"Can you find Forey and Potter for me while I'm getting your money?" Icke requested, concluding he would prefer to have his bodyguards available before going anywhere with the Indian-dark and savage-featured man.

"Sure, happen you don't mind hanging around for 'em until tomorrow at the soonest."

"Why do I have to do that?"

"They got word's how some jasper from Boston's you've sent 'em after's hid out over to Brownton 'n've took the train up there to pick up his toes like you telled 'em."

"God damn them for stupid bastards!" the receiver spat out furiously, forgetting he had given instructions for the pair to take whatever measures should prove necessary to find and kill Geoffrey Crayne. Then he was struck by another thought. Being of an untrusting persuasion, he was not enamored of the idea of sending them to retrieve his money. It was a task, he concluded, that would be best handled personally. Therefore, giving a shrug, he continued in a less hostile fashion. "Oh well, it can't be helped. If you'll wait here until I've fetched the money for you, you can show me where they're hiding and leave the rest of it to me."

"You won't get no argument with me about doing *that*," the Oklahoman declared. "Because I wasn't figuring on locking horns with 'em. They might only be women, but I'd sooner tangle with a starving grizzly b'ar than them two!"

"Are they that *dangerous*?" Icke asked, impressed by the somber way in which the comment had been made.

"Given my 'druthers,' I'd sooner pat a diamond-back rattler on its head after it's been stick-teased for the fighting pit afore I'd lock horns with them. Not less'n I'd made sure I'd got me a real good edge, anyways."

"Edge?"

"One way to do it'd be to make good 'n' sure I could get up real close without 'em knowing's how I was figuring to take them."

"How?"

"Just about the only way'd be to take out Winnie at the shack, then lay for the 'Gold-Brick' when she comes back. Trouble'd be figuring on how to do it."

"But you'd be willing to do it, if you were told a way?"

"Not for less'n a thousand simoleons," the Oklahoman claimed, his expression warning he would accept no lesser amount.

"Don't bother," Icke snorted, being unable to raise anything close to the sum quoted. However, he felt the required 'edge' he was going to suggest would work just as well for himself. Furthermore, the same objection to hiring the man in front of him applied in an even greater measure than it did where Forey and Potter were concerned, considering the amount of money he was trying to retrieve. "I'll give you fifty dollars just to show me the shack and do the rest myself."

"Make it a hundred and you've got a deal," the Oklahoman countered. "Only, afore you start figuring on doing some hoss-trading to get a lower price, leave us not forget time's a-passing, and once they get together again, you'd not have a hope in hell of taking them out."

"A hundred it is!" the receiver assented sullenly. "Wait here and I'll go fetch it for you!"

13

JUST LIKE YOU SAID, BELLE

"Right there's where the O'Toole gals're hiding out, 'Mr. Wilson,'" announced the Indian-dark Oklahoman, pointing to the small wooden shack in the poorer district of Mulrooney through which he had guided David Icke. Surrounded by a rickety picket fence, it was a short distance away from its neighbors. Only a faint glimmer of light, caused by a slight gap in the drapes drawn across the front window, suggested it might be occupied. "You mind what I've been telling you about them?"

"I'll remember everything you said," the receiver promised, but did not mention his intention to have the Oklahoman hunted down and killed by Stephen Forey and Lee Potter no matter whether he had been sold genuine or false information.

Having gone upstairs at the Railroad House Hotel, ostensibly to collect the payment for the news he had been given, Icke had been relieved to find the second-floor passage was deserted. This had allowed him to collect the woman's long, hooded black cloak from the room in which he had been drugged and robbed by "Darlene-Mae Abernathy," or—unless his informant was lying for some reason—the confidence trickster, "Gold-Brick Annie O'Toole." Taking the garment to his accommodation, he had continued his preparations for retrieving his stolen property. Laying aside his own cloak and hat, he had extracted the one-hundred-dollar bill from the hollow heel of his left Hersome gaiter boot. With the price of the information acquired, he had armed himself so as to make use of it.

Despite his frequent comments regarding the prohibition of private ownership, when addressing radical-liberal political meetings, the receiver never went anywhere without carrying at least one firearm on his person. Concluding the Remington Double Derringer—in the carefully concealed holster slot on the left side of his vest—would not be suitable for his current needs, he had taken the twin-barreled, ten-gauge, British-made Greener converted into a "whipit" gun from where it was hidden among the clothes in one of his trunks.[1] Loading the short and very deadly weapon, he wrapped it in the cloak brought from the other room and put half a dozen more buckshot shells in the right-side pocket of his jacket.

Rejoining the Oklahoman in the bar, carrying the cut-down shotgun and black cloak, the receiver had been compelled to change the one-hundred-dollar bill for notes of smaller denominations before payment was acceptable and the guidance commenced. With this done, they had left the hotel. While making their way through the semidarkness beyond the

---

1. *More detailed information regarding the kind of conversion required to produce a "whipit" gun is given in* CUT ONE, THEY ALL BLEED. *J.T.E.*

better-illuminated area of the town, the Indian-dark man had warned there was no way he could hope to arrive outside the hiding place selected by the O'Toole sisters without his presence being detected, due to certain precautions they had taken. If it was not for these, the Oklahoman had claimed, the task would be simple. Knowing her younger sister's penchant for the "pleasures of the flesh," Winnie relied upon the precautions sounding a warning and left the front door unfastened so as to avoid being disturbed when Annie returned. Asked how he knew so much, he had admitted to having been on very close terms with the less attractive sister until discarded by her after a quarrel. Pleased to have received such an interesting and helpful piece of information, Icke had concluded that the methods he intended to employ would remove the need for an unseen and unheard arrival.

"I'll give you something else for your money, being a generous son of a bitch," the Oklahoman offered. "Should you catch Winnie on her lonesome, which's likely to happen, what I recall she said about the way the 'Gold-Brick' carries on when she goes a-courting with some good-looking young jasper, you can likely take 'em one at a time and come through it alive. Was I you, though, for all you'll be wanting to put Winnie down without gunplay if you can, I'd have that sawed-off scattergun ready to use was you able to bust in on her. Don't take chances, or it'll be *you* and not her's winds up dead."

"How do you know—?" Icke began, but was unable to prevent himself from glancing at the bundle he was carrying.

"Mister," the Oklahoman drawled, having come to a halt on indicating he had brought the receiver to their destination. "You might get away with toting the scatter like you're doing it now back east, but it shows real plain to anybody's's been raised west of the Big Muddy. Which I don't blame you one li'l mite for having it. Fact being, I wouldn't want to go up against them two good ole gals, not even one at a time, any other way myself. Well, I reckon I've earned my money and it's time for me to be on my way."

"Aren't you going to wait until I've made sure they're there?"

"Nope!"

"No?"

"Mister," the Oklahoman drawled, his manner warning he would not change his mind. "I know they're there and reckon whatever comes off's between you and them. Which being, I'm going about my own doings and leaving you to your'n!"

While the final part of the conversation was taking place, never being willing to part with money unnecessarily, Icke was tempted to fell his guide the moment their separation was commenced. Then he concluded that such a course might prove to be most ill-advised. Struck from behind, the way in which the attack was to be carried out, the hat worn by the Oklahoman would offer some protection for his head. Unless he was rendered *hors de combat* by the first blow, the shack was not more than thirty yards away and the commotion that would almost certainly ensue might be heard inside. The same would also apply if the assault was successful. Furthermore, should his intentions be discovered, the receiver felt sure a painful retribution would be forthcoming immediately and his intended victim had weapons far more readily accessible than his own. Having taken the contingencies into account, therefore, he put the idea from his thoughts.

Even if Icke had elected to go ahead with his proposed attack, he would not have had the chance. Clearly having anticipated something of the kind, or possessing a natural disinclination to be trusting, the Oklahoman stepped backward until well beyond reaching distance as he was making his final declaration. Then, nodding in farewell, he swung around and strode rapidly away in the direction from which they had come.

Putting aside thoughts of trying to regain possession of the money paid for the information, the receiver told himself that he must have his bodyguard find and kill its donor. Although he had been seen to be on good terms with the beautiful blonde at the hotel, nobody else could connect him directly with the double murder he was hoping to commit. And, if the man had tricked him, he would want to have him killed as punishment.

While reaching his conclusions, Icke was unrolling the cloak from around the whipit gun. Donning the garment, he found, much to his satisfaction, that it was sufficiently voluminous to cover him from head to foot and completely hide his masculine attire. Then, although he was hoping to use it as a club rather than a firearm against at least Winnie O'Toole, he cocked both hammers before concealing the weapon by drawing the cloak around it.

On stepping forward, the receiver discovered that his informant had not lied where one point was concerned. Passing through the gate in the rickety picket fence, although there was no tree anywhere in the immediate vicinity, he found the ground was coated with dried leaves that made a noticeable crackling sound as he took a step onto them. The Oklahoman had claimed that refusing to help gather and spread them was the cause of the quarrel with the less attractive sister.

Accepting there was no way in which he could reach the building undetected, Icke walked toward it without attempting to hide. He was gambling that such a method of approach would persuade the occupant that whoever was coming had no evil intentions and did not need to worry about being overheard. As he reached the front porch without having been challenged, or seeing anything to suggest the slightest interest was being taken in him, he decided this must have been the case.

Stepping onto the porch, the receiver was startled by a creak from the sun-warped plank upon which his forward foot descended. For a moment, the glint of light at the window widened just a trifle. Although he glanced in that direction, it reverted to its original width too quickly for him to ascertain whether this was by accident or he had been subjected to observation by an occupant of the building. Deciding against taking the chance that it was the former contingency, he pulled the hood farther around his face and darted forward. Thrusting his shoulder against the door, he found that once again the Oklahoman had spoken the truth. It swung open and, starting to bring the whipit gun from beneath the cloak, without allowing his features to be displayed, he crossed the threshold swiftly.

Icke discovered, just an instant too late, that he had made a terrible mistake!

The room into which the receiver had burst was occupied, but not by the woman he had been assured would be alone!

Instead, Icke was confronted by an armed man and, from the corner of his eye, saw a second standing by the window!

What was more, both were known to the receiver!

Before Icke could disclose his identity, or do anything else to clarify the situation, the matter was taken from his hands in no uncertain fashion!

Having been told that Geoffrey Crayne was using the shack as a hiding place, but had left wearing a cloak, Forey and Potter had concluded he was searching for their employer. Satisfied that 'Mr. Wilson' could not be reached inside the Railroad House Hotel and had no intention of leaving it that night, they had elected to await the return of the young Bostonian instead of trying to locate and, perhaps, scare him off. Alerted by the crackling of the leaves and creak from the porch, Forey had peeked through the drapes. Seeing a figure dressed as had been described by their part-Indian informant, he had warned his companion to make ready.

Under the circumstances, the way selected by Icke to enter the shack could hardly have been more ill-advised!

Seeing the cloaked and unrecognizable figure burst through the door, holding a weapon offering such deadly potential at close quarters, neither of the body-guards waited to discover who it might be. Even as the receiver was trying to halt his impetuous entrance, too amazed at discovering the identity of the occupants to do anything that might have averted what was coming, the pair he had hired opened fire with their revolvers as swiftly as they could operate the single-action mechanisms.

Caught in the body by three heavy-caliber bullets, Icke was sent spinning across the room to sprawl lifeless and facedown in a corner. As he went, the whipit gun flew unheeded from his grasp. On landing, the jolt caused one of its hammers to snap forward. There was a thunderous crash, but the nine buckshot balls erupting through the cut-down barrel did nothing more than puncture a pattern of holes through the ceiling.

"Do you reckon it's him, Stevie?" Potter inquired, lowering his smoking revolver.

"Who the hell else could it be?" Forey answered, starting to walk across the room. "That goddamned half-breed, Sammy Crane, told us he was hiding out here, and how he was dressed when he went out. So let's make sure he's cashed in, then get the hell away from here."

"Maybe he's carrying money," Potter supplemented, hurrying from the window to ensure he received his fair share if this proved to be the case. "It won't do any harm to look if he is."

"Good God in heaven!" Forey exclaimed, turning the body over so that the features were revealed. His agitation was aroused less by the discovery of the victim's identity than through thoughts of how the man who had found them the job might regard their error. "What the hell's *he* doing here?"

"I dunno," Potter admitted, also staring at the lifeless features of the employer he had known only as 'Mr. Wilson.' "But we'd best light a shuck the hell from here and wonder about it later."

Leaving the shack, still holding their revolvers, the pair saw three men running toward them. Noticing the badges worn by the newcomers and the way they were armed, Potter, snarling a profanity, did not wait to be challenged. Raising his weapon, he fired and, equally perturbed by the sight, Forey duplicated his action. Neither achieved the success they had had in the building. Missing their intended marks proved to be a mistake as bad as that made by their late employer when inadvertently bursting in on them.

Each one of the approaching trio was a trained and competent peace officer, supplementing a holstered revolver with a double-barreled shotgun. Given such provocation, they retaliated swiftly. Their main armament boomed, the red flare of multiple muzzle blasts momentarily lighting the area. The discharged loads flew far more lethally than had those of the whipit gun belonging to Icke. Engulfed in the spraying cloud of .32-caliber buckshot balls, Forey was killed outright and Potter died of his wounds a few seconds later.

After having left the receiver, the tall, lean, and Indian-dark informant did not go far. Having passed only two buildings, he was confronted by three people. Two were men clad after the fashion of working cowhands. Although no longer a blonde, and now dressed more cheaply, in a style suited to the district, the other was the beautiful young woman he had claimed was the conjuneero, "Gold-Brick Annie O'Toole." There was, however, no sign of the less attractive sister, "Winnie," attributed to her.

"Howdy, Blue," greeted the female member of the trio, her voice still that of "Darlene-Mae Abernathy" except that it had lost its querulous and naive quality. "Looks like you pulled off your end, all right."

"He took the bait like a big ole bass snapping a frog offen a lily pad, Belle," the Oklahoman asserted. "How'd your end of it go down, Sammy?"

"Forey 'n' Potter're waiting for him in the shack," replied the man to whom the question was directed. His speech and appearance indicated he, too, came from Oklahoma Territory and had an admixture of Indian blood. "What I told 'em, I reckon they won't wait to do any talking when he bu'sts in on 'em."

"They haven't, I'd say!" declared the remaining cowhand, although his accent was that of a well-educated Bostonian, as the sound of shooting came from the shack. "But there was a shotgun after the revolvers. Shall we go and see if he's escaped?"

"I don't think there'll be any need for that," Belle Starr estimated. "Forey and Potter might not be what I'd call top-grade stock at gunfighting, but they know enough to be able to put down anybody who was up as close as he'd be to them when they cut loose on him."

"Yet the shotgun was fired *after* the revolvers," Geoffrey Crayne insisted, having no wish for the man he had such good reason to hate to survive the trap that had been laid by his companions.

"It was only the *one* barrel and neither of them have fired again, which they'd be too slick to be standing close enough for them both to be hit," the lady outlaw answered, being much more experienced in such matters than the man she was addressing. "If we were betting, I'd put my money on him having squeezed off when their lead hit him and didn't get either of them."

"And you'd win," claimed the man who had brought Icke from the hotel. "There's Forey 'n' Potter coming out!"

"And there's some of the town's law headed their way," warned the second Oklahoman.

"Which means it's time we were moving!" Belle stated. "Come on, Boston. You can head back home now. We've both had our revenge on David Icke."[2]

---

2. *The events recorded in the next three chapters are in the form of a "flashback." Commencing two days previous to the various activities described so far in* Part Two, *we detail the connections between Belle Starr, Geoffrey Crayne, and David Icke. J.T.E.*

14

THE MEANS FOR REVENGE

Regardless of the considerable success he had attained while playing the rugged and far-from-gentle "Boston game"—which would, despite the emphasis being more on carrying than kicking, eventually develop into the highly organized professional and amateur sporting activity known as "American football"[1]—introduced at Harvard University prior to his recent graduation, Geoffrey Crayne was not generally of a violent and vindictive nature. In fact, he had been noted for his geniality and amiable spirit when not engaged in such athletic contests or other events, to a degree that had caused his friends to declare that nothing could arouse him to anger.

---

1. *As had always been the case in the British Isles before the variant was developed at Rugby public school in 1823, and came to be called by its name, the version of football played in various universities and colleges in the United States of America at that period—sometimes with up to twenty-five men a side—allowed only kicking the ball and was much like present-day soccer. J.T.E.*

For all that, Crayne had traveled from his home in the most wealthy district of Boston, Massachusetts, to the town of Mulrooney in Kansas, with the intention of killing a man in what would almost certainly amount to cold blood.

Despite having been raised with a sound respect for law and order and the sanctity of human life, Crayne had elected to adopt such drastic action—not without considerable soul-searching—because he had reluctantly arrived at the conclusion there was no other way in which any semblance of justice could be done.

At first thought, considering the importance of his family in New England, it might have been considered Crayne would have been better advised to carry out the intended killing in, or near, his hometown. If he had, no matter how they regarded his act personally, parental influence could have been brought to bear upon his behalf and, at least, lessen the consequences created by his action. However, he had been disinclined to subject them to the adverse effects that would certainly accrue. Instead, despite knowing the risks would be greater in one respect, he had elected to make his attempt several hundred miles from New England. Unfortunately, he frequently told himself during the journey west, there would be little or no likelihood of being able to induce some kind of provocation to offer the excuse of responding in "self-defense," as such things were said to be judged in the less-than-civilized regions west of the Mississippi River.

Even more so than would have been the case back in the more adequately policed and civilized East, being the kind of man he was, David Icke would make sure he did not leave himself exposed to physical reprisals on the part of somebody who had suffered a grievous loss at his completely unscrupulous hands. However, Crayne had considered he might possibly be less upon his guard while making what he believed was a secret journey than in a region over which he had already spread his malevolent influence and incurred enmity.

Furthermore, the seeker after vengeance had concluded, there was probably a far better chance of escaping the legal penalty for his actions in Mulrooney. He would, it had occurred to him, only be in contention against rough-and-ready, casually employed peace officers who were inadequately trained for their duties, if at all. As a result, they were unlikely to be as efficient as their contemporaries in a civilized Eastern city. Their most usual adversaries were little worse than drunken cowboys who had arrived with herds of half-wild longhorn cattle from Texas, or celebrating railroad construction workers, whereas he was a sober, clear-thinking, graduate *magna cum laude* of Harvard University.

To give Crayne credit, there was much more than merely the arrogance of a college graduate behind his decision to pursue the illegal purpose that had brought him to Mulrooney. Certainly he was far from being a "liberal" intellectual of the kind who professed disdain for the processes of law and order, or sought to display an assumed superiority of intelligence over the men responsible for its enforcement. He had what he considered to be a completely justifiable reason, if not morally or legally acceptable, for having embarked upon such a course. This had nothing to do with Icke's illicit business as a receiver of stolen property; in fact, he knew nothing whatsoever about it.

Attending a party, following a political meeting of the radical variety that had grown popular with many of her friends, Andrea, Crayne's younger sister, had been raped by Icke while he was under the influence of—as he frequently asserted—harmless and even beneficial marijuana. She had then met her death as a result of having been pushed by him from a second-floor window of the house in which the affair was being held. However, so thoroughly had all traces of the festivities been removed by the wealthy "liberal" organizers, and so well had those present been induced to supply the required answers when questioned by the police, that Crayne had been informed by the investigating officers there was no way legal justice could even be set into motion, much less done.

Therefore, the young Bostonian had decided to take the law into his own hands!

To give him his due, if he had been able to acquire evidence that could have been brought before a court of law, Crayne would have been content to allow legal justice to take its course. It had for a time, in fact, seemed that he might be able to do so.

Being in a more advantageous position socially than the detectives assigned to the investigation, Crayne had persuaded one of the less culpable guests to tell him who was responsible for the death of his sister and how it had come about. As the potential witness had been on his way to give the information to the authorities, he had been knocked down and killed by a heavily loaded, apparently runaway, wagon and Crayne himself had barely escaped a similar fate. Although there was no evidence to support the theory, he had felt sure it was no accident and had been arranged either by, or at the instigation of, the man for whom he had developed an ever-growing hatred.

With the possibility of action by the police thwarted, all other potential informants having refused to talk with him, Crayne had set about seeking the means for revenge. By employing ingenuity, knowledge acquired as a student, and paying out money judiciously, he had discovered what he considered would offer the best opportunity to achieve his ends. He had learned that Icke had suddenly elected to take an unannounced trip. However, it was not known exactly where he was going or why it was felt there was a need to shroud the matter in secrecy. This seemed to rule out the possibility of a desire to further his career as author of books and plays of a most violently radical kind, or to advance his political career along similar lines. When engaged upon travels with those objectives in mind, he invariably gave advance notification of his itinerary to ensure he received adequate publicity and attention.

Nevertheless, given the knowledge of where and when he would be setting out upon the journey, trailing the intended and deserving victim had proved easy!

Now, walking through an almost deserted area of Mulrooney—given over to shipping pens for cattle and business premises concerned directly with this important factor of the town's economy—Crayne was telling himself he was ready to carry out the execution he felt was so richly deserved. Despite having been successful in following his victim, no easy opportunity of killing him presented itself.

Close to six feet in height, with a powerful build that had served him well in the rough-and-tumble play of the "Boston game" and was still kept in excellent physical condition, the vengeance seeker was in his early twenties. Wishing to avoid recognition by his proposed victim, with whom he was acquainted—albeit on far-from-amicable terms even prior to the murder of his sister—he had covered his ruggedly good-looking face with a well-made false black beard, and his reddish-brown hair was concealed by an equally realistic wig. He was further disguised in the attire of an Irish workman, such as were employed in considerable numbers to help lay down tracks for the ever-spreading tentacles of the railroad. Tucked into the waistband of his trousers, on the left side, and hidden by the unbuttoned vest of his cheap three-piece gray mottled suit, was a Colt Storekeeper Model Peacemaker. Although he had had practice with a revolver of lighter caliber, one designed for the specific purpose of firing at targets rather than as a concealable weapon, he felt he had sufficient skill at shooting to be able to produce all the accuracy he would require.

Having come from the best hotel in town, his professed desire to improve the lot of the "downtrodden working people" not extending to living among them even temporarily, Icke was strolling along the sidewalk some seventy-five yards ahead of the young Bostonian. At last he was offering an opportunity to be reached and vengeance taken.

Despite telling himself he was merely following the biblical precept of extracting an eye for an eye, as he had repeatedly been compelled to do since embarking upon his self-appointed quest for revenge, Crayne found himself wishing the distasteful and even repellent task was over. It went, he knew at the bottom of his heart, against every moral precept imparted by his Christian and law-abiding upbringing. Nor did the thought that it would soon be brought to fruition lessen the mixed emotions with which he was finding himself increasingly assailed.

Deciding to increase his pace and close the distance between them so that he could carry out his intentions, Crayne elected to leave it until he had passed two men who were standing by one of the shipping pens, studying the cattle it held. While it would be useful to have witnesses who could supply details of his present disguised appearance to the peace officers who would undoubtedly come to investigate the shooting, he did not want to be placed in the position where he might have to use the Colt against them should they try to prevent him from dealing with Icke, or stop him from escaping after the execution.

Even as the young man was reaching his conclusion, he saw Icke call, and although he could not hear what was being said, the men turned to cross the street. Halting, he concluded from various gestures being made that the author was asking for directions to somewhere. Having pointed toward the other side of the shipping pens and received nods of confirmation, Icke set off again along the sidewalk. However, instead of returning to the fence, the men started to walk in Crayne's direction.

Looking at the pair, to find out whether they were wearing badges indicating they were peace officers, the young man was not particularly interested in them. He concluded they were nothing more than cowhands killing time before making for a saloon or some other form of entertainment. Tall and lean, tanned by long hours of exposure to the elements, they had the appearance he had seen depicted in paintings of range-country activities. Nor did the low-tied holsters in which they carried their Colt Peacemakers strike him as out of the ordinary, as all the cowhands illustrated had been armed in a similar fashion.

Before Crayne and the men converged, a woman emerged from the alley he was approaching and, peering as if shortsighted, bumped into him.

About five feet eight in height, of an indeterminate age, the woman was unlikely to arouse passion unless a man had been long deprived of feminine company. Even then, this effect was only likely to be produced if there was no other member of her sex present. A "spoon bonnet," which resembled and was much the same off-yellow color as a well-weather canopy for a Conestoga wagon, was devoid of the simple decorations usually employed to brighten such drab head-gear and completely concealed her hair. Her somber and severe cheap black traveling costume was just as effective in preventing any indication of the contours inside it, other than suggesting they might be more bulky than curvaceous. Whatever good looks nature might have endowed were spoiled by a pair of large, horn-rimmed spectacles, sallow features with a some-what bulbous nose, and prominent "buck" teeth. She was grasping a furled umbrella in her right hand, and an equally bulky and shapeless black reticule was held in the left in spite of its carrying strap being around her wrist.

"Excuse me, young man!" the woman apologized, her voice a harsh and far from femininely enticing croak.

"That's all right, ma'am," Crayne replied, stepping by.

Even as he was resuming the briefly interrupted quest for revenge, the young man realized something was wrong. He had not been carrying the short-barreled, but still fairly heavy, revolver on his person for long enough to have grown so accustomed he no longer noticed its weight and bulk. Therefore, on passing the woman, he became aware that it was no longer in his waistband.

Obviously, during the momentary contact caused by the collision, the woman had stolen the weapon!

15

AS DEAD AS KELSEY'S NUTS

"Just look at this lousy Pat-Lander, Steve!"

"Yeah, Lee. Seems the hairy bastard wants to have the whole goddamned sidewalk to hisself!"

Hearing the comments made in harsh Midwest accents, as he was on the point of turning and demanding the return of the purloined revolver, Geoffrey Crayne realized that he must be the "lousy Pat-Lander" to whom the approaching men were referring with obvious hostility. Although under different circumstances he might have considered the words a tribute to his ability at adopting a convincing disguise, at that moment what he deduced from their context was a cause for some consternation. He concluded, as he was studying the demeanor of the speakers, that unless he was mistaken, they were intent upon provoking trouble. There was a truculence about them that was even more open than he had seen when confronted by a bunch of Yale students when he and some of his fraternity brothers were celebrating one evening in New York City.

However, the young man's instincts warned him that the situation might prove vastly more serious than comparatively friendly rough-and-tumble with members of what he regarded as a lesser university!

Nor was Crayne wrong!

To experienced Western eyes, Stephen Forey and Lee Potter were clearly "on the prod" and looking for trouble!

No coward, neither was the Bostonian the kind to deliberately seek trouble. Furthermore, although the term "bastard" rankled, he was less annoyed by the other remarks as he was neither Irish nor hairy. An added inducement to forbearance was that he was disinclined to let himself be turned aside from his quest for vengeance by what was nothing more than a triviality. He realized that to become involved in an unnecessary street brawl would do nothing to help him catch up with David Icke. In fact, if he should lose his false beard in a fight, his identity might be betrayed to the man he was after. Should that prove the case, being smart enough to guess what he was intending, the author would take flight and be even more difficult to approach in the future. With the latter contingency in mind, he decided he would not allow himself to be provoked by the two men.

A person better acquainted with the West than Crayne would have read something vastly more sinister than an attempt to start a fistfight in the behavior of Forey and Potter. Halting so as to block the sidewalk, despite being about four feet apart, each was holding his right hand with seeming negligence close to the butt of his low-tied revolver. It was the posture of a frontier-trained gunfighter at readiness to draw and throw lead.

Wondering whether the two men were in league with the woman who had purloined his revolver, Crayne decided against putting the matter to the test.

He would do all he could to avoid trouble. On the point of doing so, he was given the biggest surprise of his life.

"Pathrick Moichael O'Toole!" yelled a feminine voice with a strong Irish brogue. "Don't yez dast go picking no foight with them cowboys. Didn't yez bust up two of 'em just the day ago and wasn't it meself's had to bail you out of jail?"

Hearing the words and seeing the woman who had collided with the Easterner stalking past him, Forey and Potter exchanged glances redolent of puzzlement!

The effect that the announcement had upon the hard cases was nothing compared to the amazement aroused in Crayne. Not only had the speaker stolen his revolver during their brief moment of contact, but, although she was a complete stranger, she now seemed to be mistaking him for a close acquaintance, or even someone related to her. However, something else occurred to him as she began to turn his way. There had been no trace of the broad Irish accent in the few words she had addressed to him when she had apologized for the collision.

After staring at the woman for a moment, Forey and Potter again traded puzzled looks. Then the taller of them gave a jerk with his head in her direction and, indicating himself with a jerk of his left thumb, nodded toward the Bostonian.

"All right, you goddamned peat bog biddy!" Potter growled, stepping forward in accordance with the signals he had received and laying his left hand on the shoulder of the female intruder. "Get the h—!"

The words came to an end as the woman exhibited resentment at being spoken to, and treated, in such a fashion. Twisting her shoulder free and grasping the bulky umbrella in both hands—having dropped her reticule before moving forward—she pivoted with more grace than might have been expected of one with her somewhat dumpy build. Thrusting as she turned, she rammed the curved handle hard just above the waistband of the shorter hard case. Giving a startled profanity, he stumbled backward a few steps.

Relying upon his companion to take care of the intruder, Forey had walked past her alert for any movement on the part of the Bostonian that would offer an excuse to pull and use his gun. Concentrating upon his intended victim, although he heard the pain-filled exclamation from Potter, he was not granted an opportunity to investigate.

Showing the same kind of speed as when dealing with the shorter hard case, the woman swung around. Sending her right hand to join the left lower on the umbrella, she reached and hooked its handle into the back of Forey's open-necked shirt. Having done so, she gave a swinging heave. Caught unawares and with one foot off the ground in midstep, the strength with which he was assailed caused him to be spun away from his intended victim. Unable to stop himself, before he could even so much as utter a sound in protest, he felt the handle removed and was propelled across the sidewalk. Striking the hitching rail, he went over in a half-somersault to alight on his back in the street.

Watching in openmouthed astonishment, everything happening so rapidly he could not catch up with the event, Crayne found himself unable to respond despite seeing the woman was being threatened by the shorter hard case. Face suffused by rage, Potter was starting toward her with the obvious intention of avenging the blow he had taken. Showing an awareness of the possibility, she reacted to it in a swift and positive fashion. Turning, with her hands moving apart on the umbrella, she employed it as a soldier would a bayonet by jabbing with the steel ferrule at the point already struck by the handle. The effect was even more severe, but it was not the only suffering she inflicted. Withdrawing the ferrule, she swung it upward to catch him under the chin. Back snapped his head and, as he blundered away from his assailant, it struck the wall of the building at the other edge of the sidewalk. Stunned by the impact, he crumpled limply to the planks.

Despite being partially winded by the fall, Forey was sitting up. Mouthing breathless profanities, he reached with his right hand and found only the empty top of his holster. Looking around, he located the revolver that had fallen from it as he was passing over the hitching rail. More eager to take revenge upon the cause of his misfortunes than to settle accounts with the Easterner, he made a grab. Just before his fingers could close around the butt, he once more felt his collar seized by the crook of the umbrella. On this occasion, however, the jerk it delivered drove the base of his skull against the edge of the sidewalk and he too was rendered unconscious.

"What in God's name is going on?" Crayne asked, having stood transfixed by astonishment over what he was witnessing. "I've never seen you before in my life!"

"I know you haven't," the woman agreed, and her voice had become that of a well-educated Southron. Strolling by, she retrieved the reticule she had dropped in order to have the full use of both hands. Opening its neck, she reached inside to produce the short-barreled revolver placed there after taking it from its owner. "Here, but if you're carrying it for what I think you may be, you'd best forget it."

"I don't know wha—!" the Bostonian began.

Reminded of what had brought him to Mulrooney, the remarkable behavior of the woman having momentarily driven it from his thoughts, Crayne looked around. He discovered that David Icke had stopped and was watching what was happening. Finding himself under scrutiny, the author turned and hurried away.

"Not for *that*!" the woman stated, withdrawing the revolver as the young man turned and reached toward it. "I don't know what's between you and him, but he knows you're after him. That's why he led you here, so Forey and Potter could *stop* you."

"*Stop?*" the young Bostonian gasped, having noticed the particular emphasis placed upon the word and realizing what it might have been used to imply. Looking from one to the other of the men he had thought were nothing more than chance-met cowboys, then staring again at his rescuer, he went on, "You mean they meant—?"

"They for sure weren't just a couple of cowhands on the prod against Pat-Landers," the woman asserted with complete assurance, glancing around in a way that reminded the young man of a wary wild creature surveying its surroundings for potential danger. "Fact being, as soon as you'd made anything like a move toward this cut-down Peacemaker of yours—or even if you didn't make one—they'd have shot you down as dead as Kelsey's nuts."

"I—I don't *understand*!" Crayne croaked, staring at the speaker as if hardly able to accept the evidence of his eyes, much less what she had just done and was now saying.

"If I give you your Colt back," the woman drawled, darting glances about her, "will you give me your word that you'll come with me and wait until you've heard me out before you try to commit *murder* with it?"

"*Murder?*" The Bostonian repeated, the full ugly implication of the word striking him as it had failed to do previously.

"*Murder,*" the woman reiterated. "Could be I've called the play wrong, but I reckon that's what it would've come down to should you have been let catch up with—!"

"How did you *know*?" Crayne croaked, his voice hoarse, staring at the revolver being held in his direction.

"That beard and wig look real enough," the woman explained, glancing to where her two victims were beginning to stir and show signs of regaining consciousness. "But I made them out as fakes as soon as I saw you and, going by this pair of choice *pistoleros* having been told to lay for and make wolf bait of you, so did Buckton."

"Buckton?"

"Hell, yes. Likely you'd know the son of a bitch as 'David Icke.' "

"I do, but I still don't understand—!"

"You will soon enough," the woman promised, making a gesture with the Colt. "Well, do I have your word that you'll come along and hear me out if you take this?"

"Why should I give you my word about *anything*?" Crayne challenged, despite a growing belief that he was not talking to an ordinary person and concluding she was unlike any other member of her sex he had met. Looking to where he had last seen the man he was intending to kill, he found only an area devoid of all human life. "Oh damn it. He's *gone*—!"

"You can easy enough find him again, should you still be *loco* enough to want to," the woman pointed out, an edge of impatience and annoyance having come into a voice that suggested much more grace and glamour than was implied by her appearance. "But that's all the way left up to *you*."

"Then why are you here?" the Bostonian asked, realizing this was unlikely to have come about by chance.

"I'll answer all your questions, but not here and

now," the woman promised, her manner indicating she was adamant on the matter. "Marshall Kail Beauregard's as honest a peace officer's could have been found to take over the badge from Dusty Fog,[1] but I'm not overeager to have him asking me the why-for I took down those two yahoos while I'm wearing a disguise the same as you are. So make your choice and *pronto*, mister. Take your gun and come with me, or go *try* to do what you've come to Mulrooney for. Either way, I'm lighting a shuck away before the marshal or his deputies get here, or Forey and Potter come 'round and have to be quietened down again."

"I—I'll come with you," Crayne decided, accepting the Colt and returning it to his waistband. Accompanying the woman away from the two slowly recovering hard cases, he went on, "How do you know David Icke and, if you don't mind me asking, who are you?"

"My name is Belle Starr," the rescuer of the Easterner introduced, reversing the order in which the information was requested.

---

1. *The events that led to and followed the appointment of Captain Dustine Edward Marsden "Dusty" Fog, q.v., as town marshal of Mulrooney, Kansas, are recorded in* THE MAKING OF A LAWMAN, THE TROUBLE BUSTERS, *and* THE GENTLE GIANT. *Two incidents during the time in office of Town Marshall Kail Beauregard are described in* WHITE STALLION, RED MARE, *and* THE WHIP AND THE WAR LANCE. J.T.E.

16

I Know Who He Was

"*Belle Starr?*" Geoffrey Crayne interrupted, before the first part of his question could be answered, remembering the colorful accounts of various illicit activities attributed to the bearer of that name he had read in newspapers and magazines. Staring in something akin to disbelief at the woman he did not doubt had saved him from serious injury and, if she had spoken the truth, perhaps even death, he went on, "But I've always heard you were beauti— They say you're a *criminal!*"

"And what they say is true, whoever *they* might be," the lady outlaw admitted without shame or annoyance, regarding the slighting reference to her appearance as a tribute to her skill in adopting a disguise.[1] "In fact, being a *criminal* is how I came to know the man you're after."

---

1. *Another occasion when Belle Starr made use of such an unflattering disguise, albeit without the false "buck" teeth, is recorded in* THE GENTLE GIANT. *J.T.E.*

"You *know* David Icke?"

"I know of him as 'David Icke'—And I know who he *was* too!"

"Who he *was*?" the young Bostonian queried, sensing from the way the comment had been made that the knowledge was not pleasant for the woman walking by his side.

"Back in those days, he was calling himself 'Raymond Buckton,'" Belle explained, her tone bitter under its otherwise cultured Southern drawl. "He was one of those carpetbagger scum who came crawling like lice into the Indian Nations and all through the South after the war, looting and relying for protection on Yankee blue-bellies led by the likes of Smethurst—!"

"Do you mean the General Smethurst who was murdered by the Ku Klux Klan not too long ago?" Crayne inquired, allowing himself to be guided away from the area given over to cattle shipping pens and toward what appeared to be the poorer section of Mulrooney without anybody challenging their right to depart.

"The same, except that it wasn't *murder*," the lady outlaw confirmed definitely. "And, although I don't doubt that the Klan would have counted it an honor to have rid the world of him, they didn't do it."[2]

"What did Ic—Buckton—do to you?" Crayne asked, deciding there was nothing to be gained by discussing such an emotive subject further and being more interested in finding the connection with the man for whom he had developed so great a hatred.

"Nothing personally!"

"Then why—?"

"He had himself appointed as Land Commissioner,

---

2. *How and why General Wilbur B. Smethurst, United States Army, was killed is told in* THE HOODED RIDERS. *J.T.E.*

or some such fancy title, for the Muskogee district of the Nations and he surely showed us Johny Rebs what Yankee Reconstruction meant. Folks were made to sell off their land for a fraction of its worth, supposedly to be used as farms for freed slaves; although none ever came and it wound up being owned by white Yankees."

"There was more to it than just that, though?" Crayne hinted, being sufficiently fair-minded to concede there had been many injustices perpetrated upon Southrons in the name of Reconstruction.

"Plenty more," Belle agreed. "Those who wouldn't sell peaceably were run off, or killed by his men. One of the families who wouldn't sell and didn't run were real close kin of mine. Buckton got liquored up one night and led the bunch who went to wipe them out. Way I heard it, it was him who shot down my aunt Mae as she was kneeling by Uncle Benjamin and was laughing as he did it."

"So you're after revenge against him, too?" the Bostonian stated, rather than just asked.

"I'm after revenge against him, too," the lady outlaw admitted, and something in the gentle-sounding words caused the young man to feel as if a chilly hand was running along his spine. The sensation made him grateful that she was not after his blood. "But not only for what happened back in the Nations, since I saw and recognized him at the railroad depot."

"How do you mean?"

"I didn't know he was Land-Grabber Buckton until then!"

"I'm sorry," Crayne said. "But I don't follow you!"

"There were some decent and fair dealing bluebelly officers as well as Smethurst and his kind," Belle elaborated. "They found out what Buckton was up to and aimed to have him arrested, but he lit a shuck before they could lay hands on him and was thought to have drowned crossing the Arkansas River while it was running in flood. That's why I never tried to find him and it handed me one hell of a surprise when I found he was the 'David Icke' who I'd come down here to meet."

"*You* had come to meet Icke?"

"Yes."

"But how—?"

"Quite easily. I got word to him that there was some very good jewelry for sale, but he'd have to come to Mulrooney to pick it up."

"Jewelry?"

"He buys it, among other things, from people like me."

"I'm sorry, Miss Starr. Perhaps I'm dense, but I still don't understand. Icke's an author, a playwright, and a politician—!"

"So I've heard," Belle drawled. "All of which helps him to be one of the biggest fences in the U.S. of A."

"*Fence?*" the Bostonian queried, this being a day and age before the language of the underworld had become public knowledge.

"That's what folks like me called the fellers who buy the things we steal," the lady outlaw explained, deciding the young man really did not know what was meant by "fence" in such a context and concluding she was wrong with regard to his reason for seeking revenge against Icke."In fact, two very good friends of mine, who'd got hold of some bonds and other stuff while they were making a visit back east, were sent to sell it to him. Only, when they wouldn't take the piker's offer he made them, he fixed it so they were caught by the police and they're still in jail."

"Why didn't they tell the police about him?" Crayne inquired.

"That's something we don't do, at least not friends of mine, *anyways*," Belle replied, feeling sure her companion was not a criminal. "On top of which, they'd never met him face-to-face or even learned his real name, the one he's using now. It took me some time to find out who he was. When I did, I fixed it to have him come out here on my home range so I could teach him a lesson."

"You meant to have him killed?"

"Not then."

"Then?"

"Like I said, I didn't know he was Buckton until I saw him get down from the train," Belle answered quietly, but did not mention she had noticed the young Easterner disembarking and guessed he was wearing a disguise for some reason. "Only now it isn't just going to stop with taking the money he's brought to pay for the jewelry. I'm going to pay him back in *full* for what he did to Aunt Mae and Uncle Benjamin."

"Now I understand!" Crayne asserted. "Some of it, anyway."

"And how about you?" the lady outlaw wanted to know, studying as much of the young man's face as was left visible by the false beard. "You're from Boston, by your accent, and I don't reckon you're after him because he's done dirt to you, or somebody close to you, as a fence."

"No, that isn't why I'm after him," the Bostonian replied vehemently and told of his reason for following Icke, concluding, "And, as the law couldn't touch him, I swore I'd make him pay myself for what he'd done to Andrea."

"So you aimed to just walk up and blow blue windows in him with that Colt, did you?"

"Yes!"

"In *cold blood?*"

"He wouldn't let it happen any other way," Crayne claimed. "Even if dueling was still legal, he'd never have had the guts to face me man to man."

"Likely not," Belle conceded. "Only, seeing it would be *murder* no matter how well justified you are in your reason, I don't think you'd have been able to go through with it if the time had come."

"Why not?" the Bostonian demanded, although he had had similar thoughts on the matter. "He deserves to die for what he did to my sister."

"I'm not gainsaying *that*," the lady outlaw said gently.

"But you don't think I'd have the courage to do it?"

"You're not a coward and I never even started to think you might be. But it takes a special breed of man to *murder* in cold blood, and if I reckoned you were that kind, I wouldn't be walking with you this way."

"You may be right about how I'd have acted," Crayne sighed, concluding from the way in which his companion had just spoken that—despite being a criminal—she had scant regard for the kind of person who would be willing to kill in the manner he had contemplated.

"I *know* I'm right," Belle claimed, having taken a liking to the young man and wanting to ensure he was aware of the enormity of the act he had intended to commit. "I've grown up and spent most of my life among men, good and bad, who've had to kill. One thing I've learned is how to tell the kind who can *murder* in cold blood, and you aren't one of them. So I hope you'll be willing to leave Buckt—Icke— to me."

"But you're only a wom—!" the Bostonian began.

"I know I'm 'only' a woman," the lady outlaw drawled, showing no offense at what had almost been said. "But being one is why I'll be able to get to and at him."

On the point of asking how his companion intended to wreak her revenge upon the person they both had such good reason to hate, the attention of the young Bostonian was divested from the subject.

Two men had come from a small saloon a short distance ahead of the couple. Although their black hair was cut short, they had aquiline coppery brown features that reminded Crayne of paintings he had seen depicting Indians and were, he guessed, indicative of an admixture of blood with that race. Tall and lean, they were dressed after the fashion of Texas cowboys. In addition to the holstered Colt, each also carried a sheathed knife on his gunbelt.

After looking at the woman and the Bostonian for a moment, the Indian-dark pair exchanged low-spoken comments. Then, stepping from the sidewalk, they started to stroll forward. Nonchalant as it seemed, Crayne considered there was something vaguely menacing about the prowling manner in which they were moving. They looked wary and alert, as if ready to take whatever action might become necessary without a moment's hesitation.

"What's wrong?" Belle inquired, having noticed the change that had come over her companion.

"Those two men coming this way!" Crayne hissed, looking at the lady outlaw and holding down his voice. "They look *dangerous*!"

"They are *dangerous*!"

"Are they working for Icke?"

"No, they're good friends of mine. Hey there, Sammy, Blue, come and meet this gent from Boston, Massachusetts. You'll find he doesn't care for good ole Land-Grabber Buckton any more than we do, except he knows him as 'David Icke.' "

"Now, that sounds like you're a feller with real good sense," announced the taller of the pair, Blue Duck, his accent that of an Oklahoman and only slightly guttural. "What do you reckon, *amigo*?"

"I'll float my stick along of you, Blue," Sammy

Crane replied, his manner of speech indicative of similar origins. "Did you see good ole Land-Grabber, Belle?"

"I've seen him," the lady outlaw confirmed, as the pair started walking along with her and the Easterner.

"I hopes he looked in good spirits," Blue Duck drawled, but without any noticeable sincerity in his voice.

"He looked spry and happy," Belle declared. "Where're you bedding down, Boston?"

"At a small rooming house not far from the railroad depot," Crayne answered. "And my name is—!"

"Just 'Boston' will do for us," the lady outlaw interrupted, but in a friendly manner. "Anyways, he probably knows you went there. So we'd best get you moved out. Or, better still, if you don't have anything you value and need in your room, you can stay away altogether."

"I don't have anything I need. At least, nothing that can't be replaced," Crayne asserted. Knowing he would have to take flight immediately, if he succeeded in his purpose, he had realized the futility of bringing anything of value that could help trace him should he make good his escape. "But I don't want to leave Mulrooney until I'm su—until after I've seen what happens to Icke."

"That's all right with me," Belle accepted, and pointed to a small wooden shack standing slightly away from its neighbors. "That's where we're staying. It isn't luxurious, but it's clean and, if you're so minded, you can move in with us—provided you're willing to leave handling Buckt—Icke to *me*."

"You've got a deal, Miss Starr," the Bostonian declared without hesitation.

17

HOW IT WAS DONE

Even before coming to the rescue of Geoffrey Crayne, whom, at her own insistence, she never knew other than as "Boston," Belle Starr had been engaged upon the preliminaries to extract vengeance upon David Icke for the betrayal and imprisonment of her friends. Putting to use the facilities available to her, she had learned all she could about her intended quarry and, based upon this information, had selected from her extensive repertoire of schemes those she had felt best suited to her needs. The active stages of the preparations had been commenced two days before the arrival in Mulrooney of the receiver and his other pursuer. However, she had not settled upon the exact method to be used until after they had come.

With the supposed offer of the stolen jewelry for sale having been accepted, the robbery having taken place although the identity of the outlaws responsible was still not known, the lady outlaw had traveled to the town she designated as rendezvous with Icke. To establish the character she would be playing, she had booked by telegraph a room at the Railroad House Hotel in the name "Darlene-Mae Abernathy." She had arrived complete with a blond wig, suitable clothing, and baggage, letting it be believed she had come— accompanied by her maid—to attend to a business matter for her very wealthy family in Richmond, Virginia. This had allowed her to appear, as the occasion demanded, in two different guises inside and out of the hotel.[1]

The intervening period had been spent by Belle in making the contacts necessary for whichever deception she finally selected. Being the most complex, those involving the National Trust Bank had demanded most of her attention. In fact, having satisfied herself it offered what she needed, she had intended to make sure of it in another direction if Icke did not play the part she planned for him. Her shrewd assessment had helped her select which of the tellers would best suit her purpose. Telling Cyrus B. Cockburn that she was instructed by her family to look over various properties in the vicinity with a view to purchase, she had persuaded him to let Dennis Hobert accompany her to inspect such prospects as might prove of interest.

For obvious reasons, Belle had been compelled to

---

1. *On checking into the Railroad House Hotel in her character as "Darlene-Mae Abernathy," Belle Starr had informed the desk clerk that the maid she had accompanying her was occupying cheaper accommodation elsewhere, but would be bringing her luggage and coming each day to attend to her needs. Leaving instructions for the nonexistent maid at the reception desk, announcing she was taking a stroll to see the sights, she had joined Blue Duck and Sammy Crane. Donning the appropriate disguise, she had returned to the hotel as promised. By careful manipulation, she had contrived to maintain the two different identities without the deception being discovered. J.T.E.*

adopt her less flattering appearance when visiting the railroad depot to keep watch for the man she was awaiting, who was descending from a westbound train. Being something of an authority where such matters were concerned, it had taken more than the removal of a beard and mustache, plus the addition of a few years, to prevent her from recognizing a hated face from the past.

The biggest surprise for the lady outlaw had come from learning that the murderer of her aunt and uncle was also the receiver she had enticed to Mulrooney. It was a discovery that had led her to change her motives and ultimate goal. She had been merely going to fleece him of the money that he had brought in response to her story and any other valuables he might have in his possession, by means calculated to cause him great humiliation when she sent news of it to his home territory. Instead, she had elected to inflict a much more severe penalty. However, in the earlier stages, she had not needed to revise her *modus operandi* on account of the proposed victim having proved to be Raymond "Land-Grabber" Buckton, the erstwhile scourge of Oklahoma.

Having noticed the young Bostonian and his obvious interest in her quarry, although willing to admit it required the most experienced eye to detect the "hair" and "beard" he was wearing were false, Belle had first thought he might be a criminal with a similar desire for revenge against the receiver. Wanting to deal with "Mr. Wilson" personally—particularly after having realized his other alias—and not wishing him to be frightened off by a bungled attempt on his life, or through discovering he had been followed from the east by an enemy, she had had Blue Duck and Sammy Crane help her keep Crayne under observation.

Handling the surveillance of the Bostonian at the

time, the lady outlaw had followed ready to prevent him from using the revolver he was carrying to kill Icke. Seeing Stephen Forey and Lee Potter waiting in the almost deserted shipping pens district, aware that they were acting as bodyguards for the receiver, she had realized Crayne was being led into a trap. Contriving to pass around the rear of the buildings, unnoticed by any of the men, she had appeared in a position to prevent the Bostonian from falling into it. He had then remained in the care of her two companions. Dressed after the fashion of a cowhand from Texas, but taking care never to speak where they could hear him, he had on two occasions been close to Forey and Potter during their search for him and they had not suspected their quarry was so near.

Although Belle had been considering more than one scheme for achieving her original purpose, any of which would have served even in the new circumstances, she had finally elected to use the confidence trick involving the National Trust Bank. She had had another potential "mark" in mind for it, in fact, but changed her objective when she discovered Icke had deposited the money in the vault. Ensuring he saw her in the company of the young man he knew to be a teller at that establishment, having concocted a satisfactory story to explain why their supposed relationship was not known if the matter should be raised, she had set the scheme into operation. She remembered how "Buckton" had acquired a reputation for lecherous proclivities in Oklahoma. According to her information about Icke from sources in the East and from Crayne, these remained unchanged. Therefore, she had felt sure "Darlene-Mae Abernathy" would be sufficiently attractive for him to be willing to exploit the situation where she was concerned, under the pretense of helping her "half brother."

With the other preparations made, and having

ascertained that Hobert was ambitious, not overburdened with scruples or loyalty to his employer, the
lady outlaw had had no difficulty in ensuring he
would be absent from the bank at the appropriate
time. At her instigation, he had sent a message
claiming a sudden attack of grippe would prevent him
from coming into work. He had then set off to inspect a property some fifteen miles from Mulrooney,
having been led to believe the "Abernathy family"
were interested in it and that he would be a benefi-
ciary, rather than the banker, should a successful deal
for its purchase be concluded.

Knowing that Icke was staying close to the hotel,
waiting to hear from the outlaws bringing the stolen
jewelry, Belle had intended to call at his room to tell
her story. However, seeing him coming into the
reception lobby while on her way to his room, she
had taken the opportunity to intercept him. The com-
petence of her acting had achieved the desired effect
and he had set off with the intention of retrieving the
money he had deposited before it could be impounded. Being aware that the elderly teller had no
liking for his younger and more forceful colleague,
she had counted upon his annoyance over any work
caused by the absence to produce an attitude suited
to her needs when the receiver arrived. Although she
did not know, her efforts had succeeded.

Having followed the scheme through to where it
would have ended under her original plan, and leaving
the hotel with all the valuable loot in her possession,
the lady outlaw had set into motion the revisions
required as a result of the changed circumstances.
Learning of what had happened to Andrea Crayne had
merely strengthened her resolve and made her all the
more determined to put through the new portion of
the plan.

Waiting outside at the time it had been estimated

the effects of the drugged drink would wear off, Blue Duck had contacted Icke on his appearance in the lobby. His reaction to the story about "Gold-Brick Annie and Winnie O'Toole" had been as was anticipated. Belle had guessed he would prefer to retrieve his property personally, rather than trust the task to his bodyguards or the man who had brought him the "information." However, in case she had been wrong, he was led to assume neither bodyguard would be available that evening, and was quoted a higher price than he could afford for obtaining the services of Blue Duck. Knowing his publicly stated abhorrence of firearms—ownership was far from a true condition where he personally was concerned—she had felt sure he would have weapons available to be used in the attempt. She had also done something that, it was hoped, would help bring about the desired result.

Going to Forey and Potter, Sammy Crane had told them where the man they were seeking could be located and, if absent when they arrived, how he was likely to be dressed on his return. Shortly before their employer was brought to the shack by Blue Duck, they were inside with the intention of carrying out his orders by disposing of the young Bostonian.

Having avoided being seen by the receiver as he passed with his informant, the other conspirators had concluded he was taking very seriously what he had been told about the dangerous qualities of the "O'Toole sisters." He had been wearing the woman's cloak, deliberately left in the wardrobe by the lady outlaw, hoping it would enable him to reach the building in a less suspicious manner than with his masculine attire showing. However, even if he had not adopted such a line of action, bursting in upon the waiting pair holding the whipit gun, it was unlikely he would have been given an opportunity to clarify the situation before they started shooting.

As it was, everything had gone as Belle wished!

A honest and upright young man had been saved from committing an act that—even if he had not been caught, tried, and hanged—would have ruined his life!

For her part, although she later had to dispose of the "hot" money in a fashion she had not anticipated on acquiring it, the lady outlaw was adequately recompensed for the time and expense of the scheme. Having had the contents of the pocketbook deciphered, she arranged for the withdrawal of the bank accounts kept by the receiver under assumed names. Furthermore, she had taken an appropriate revenge upon a man who had fully deserved what happened to him at her instigation.

Legal justice had been unable to touch David Icke, even in his previous identity of "Raymond 'Land-Grabber' Buckton," but retribution had come to him at the hands of Belle Starr.

PART THREE

BIRDS OF A FEATHER

18

I'VE HEARD THAT ONE *BEFORE*

Noticing that the cashier of the Crystal Room Café was looking pointedly in his direction, after having spoken with the couple who had earlier asked him to be their guest at what must have proved to be a most costly lunch, Hubert Charles Penfold the Third assumed the cashier was being informed that his host would settle the check on their return to the café. Nodding and giving a confirmatory wave with his pudgy right hand, he settled back on his chair in self-satisfied contentment. Taken all in all, he considered the events of the day were combining to make his visit to Fort Worth, Texas, more lucrative than he had originally envisaged.

Tallish, brown-haired, and in his late thirties, Penfold was bulky albeit in a soft-fleshed fashion. His somewhat porcine features invariably bore an expression he considered to be masterful, but only made it appear he was smelling an unpleasant odor. Currently, his face was far from improved by having the skin peeled due to being exposed to a much stronger sun than that to which he was accustomed in Pittsburgh, Pennsylvania. Although somber in color and devoid of everything he considered to be "frivolous adornments," his clothing was cut from the best-quality materials and in the latest Eastern style.

Imbued by wealthy and overindulgent parents with a sense of his own importance and superiority to those about him, Penfold nevertheless prided himself upon being a "stout and upright" Christian. To ensure this sterling quality was not overlooked, having discovered there were many advantages to having people believe he possessed it, he never left anybody for long unaware of it and frequently found reasons for declaring his unswerving adherence to the doctrines of the Eastern Traditional Baptist Church. He had selected this particular sect because, while expanding its numbers, little enough was generally known about its particular beliefs for him to be caught out when he wished to use it advantageously.

Regardless of his numerous pronouncements, Penfold did not carry his boasted Christian precepts to any excessive length when dealing with others. As was being demonstrated by his activities that day, although ready and willing to produce something that sounded like a religious reason for his behavior, he was far from overburdened by scruples. After a lesser piece of luck a short while earlier, he considered he was now being offered a chance to turn a healthy profit his way.

On leaving his room at the Cattlemen's Hotel, with the intention of asking at the reception desk on the ground floor whether any messages had arrived for him, Penfold had seen an expensive-looking wallet lying in the passage near the head of the stairs. Picking it up, he had ascertained that it contained twenty dollars in bills and what was, in all probability, the name and address of its owner. Hearing the door of a nearby room being opened, he had tucked the wallet into a pocket of his jacket and hurriedly set off downstairs instead of waiting to learn who was coming into the passage.

Being a firm advocate of "finders keepers, losers weepers," although asserting in exculpation that the Good Lord disapproved of negligence with those gifts provided by His bounty, Penfold had no intention of trying to return the wallet to its rightful owner. Therefore, should it be the owner who was coming from the room, he had no desire to be seen and questioned on the subject. Should he have been asked if he had seen the wallet, he would have to admit this was the case. However, by his own standard, unless such an inquiry was made he would be at liberty to keep it.

Glancing over his shoulder on reaching the ground floor, Penfold satisfied himself that nobody was in sight. Nor was the lobby occupied, even the reception desk being unmanned, as he strode to the front entrance. Stepping outside, he watched a couple descending whom he had noticed without giving them any great attention, in the dinning room the previous evening. They were as somberly dressed as himself. Not only did the man wear the "reversed" collar of many denominations' clergy, but his face was leathery and suggestive of a harsh religious fervor. Everything about the demeanor of the much younger woman implied that such was his nature. Although beautiful, there was little about her to arouse the "baser passions." Her pallid features were marred by horn-rimmed spectacles and an expression of cowed, down-trodden meekness. Whatever curves her figure might possess were completely hidden beneath a shapeless black dress, and a plain poke bonnet concealed every vestige of her hair. Following upon the heels of her male companion, clutching a bulky black reticule as if afraid it would be snatched from her, her head hung forward and her whole bearing was redolent of subservience.

Satisfied it would be assumed he was just returning to the hotel, Penfold had entered and crossed to the desk. He arrived in time to hear the gaunt man asking whether there were any Eastern Traditional Baptists in Fort Worth. Although Penfold had for once no intention of admitting his connection with the creed, in case it resulted in a request for a donation to the church, the clerk had pointed him out. Despite his annoyance at having been identified, the anticipated suggestion of a subscription had not been made. Instead, much to his surprise, he had received an invitation to join the couple for a meal. Not at the hotel, either, but in the best and most expensive café offered by Fort Worth. However, having had much to do with members of his creed, he had suspected there would be more behind the offer than merely a desire for his company.

The supposition had proved correct!

While waiting in the comfortable foyer for a table to become vacant, the gaunt man had introduced himself as "Pastor Samuel Salford" and, clearly as an afterthought, said the younger woman was his daughter, Alice. Then he had explained that he was faced with a problem. In the throes of religious uplift and exaltation, a recent convert to their mutual creed had donated a desirable piece of property along the Trinity River to be sold for the funds of the church. There had been a stipulation. Considering nobody else would be sufficiently honest, the sale could be handled only by an Eastern Traditional Baptist. As it had been known Salford would be passing through Fort Worth on his way to Austin, he was delegated to make the negotiations. Unfortunately, due to a mix-up in the arrangements, the matter could not be concluded until the following day and he must leave on the afternoon stagecoach if he was to bring to a desirable conclusion the most important business that was taking him to the state capitol.

Never willing to put himself out for others, unless seeing a way in which he might benefit personally from doing so, Penfold had listened without interest until hearing there were three potential purchasers involved. Furthermore, each had expressed an eagerness to buy, which was not unexpected considering the far-from-exorbitant price at which the land had been offered. This could have been raised considerably without deterring the intended buyers, the Pastor had asserted, even though the elders of the church had expressed concurrence with the figure quoted.

Concluding he could obtain the higher price by persuading the would-be purchasers to bid against one another, then pocketing the difference without mentioning it to the elders, Penfold hesitated to make an offer to take over the negotiations. He had met too many men like the Pastor, and he felt sure such a suggestion would arouse suspicion and be refused. He wondered how he might bring about the proposal. The matter was taken from his hands by the young woman, making her first contribution to the conversation in a Southern drawl as meek and submissive as that of her father's was harsh and domineering. She pointed out that their guest was also an Eastern Traditional Baptist and was qualified to make the sale.

However, Penfold considered the remark made by Alice a mixed blessing. The Pastor, being the kind of man he was, resented her intervention. Growling that they knew nothing about their guest, he refused to be mollified by his daughter claiming Mr. Penfold looked honest. Eager to be given the task, the young man produced his wallet and displayed fifteen hundred

dollars. Conceding this was evidence of financial sound-
ness, Salford suggested a test of his honesty. Producing a thick pocketbook from inside his black
jacket, the Pastor presented it to Penfold with the
instruction that it should be taken outside for a few
minutes. Its safe return, Salford declared, would be
sufficient to satisfy him upon this most important
point.

Having no doubt that to refuse was almost certain
to preclude him from further participation in the
affair, Penfold concluded it would be advisable to
humor his host and accepted the terms. While strolling around the café building, he examined the contents of the pocketbook. His hope of learning more
about the negotiations over the property failed to
materialize. It had held five hundred dollars and a
letter informing Salford that a new church in the most
wealthy part of Austin required an incumbent, but
there was nothing about the sale of the property.
Deciding he had at least discovered why his host was
in such a hurry to reach the state capitol, he had
returned and found the couple were already seated in
the dining room.

Approaching the table, Penfold overheard the
young woman making a remark to the effect that there
would hardly be sufficient time. However, becoming
aware of his presence at that moment, Salford prevented her from continuing. Nevertheless, on sitting
down, the young man soon began to suspect the
nature of the interrupted comment. Having accepted
the pocketbook and, without apology, checked that its
contents were intact, the Pastor showed no inclination
to start discussing the reason for it having been taken
away. In fact, he became evasive when Penfold tried to
raise the matter of the sale. To the young man's way of
thinking, the reticence suggested that his host had
belatedly seen the possibility of making a personal

profit from the deal and was considering delaying his departure for Austin to conduct the business himself.

Having met a number of men like Salford, Penfold knew better than to ask directly for the deeds to be handed over so he could handle the ensuing deal. Remembering the letter in the pocketbook, his devious and not overscrupulous mind suggested a solution to the problem. The writer had warned that, not having made their acquaintance or being known to any of them, the Pastor would have to create a suitable impression with the Elders responsible for appointing the incumbent. Penfold therefore told the Pastor that he had met the Elders in question and, without mentioning the lucrative post that he knew was available, he said the thing that had struck him most about them was their insistence upon strict punctuality in all matters pertaining to the business of the Church.

Despite having clearly taken what he was told to heart, it was obvious that Salford still hoped to find a reason to remain in Fort Worth and personally conclude the profitable negotiations. At last, with the meal over, he declared that real trust could only be established by proof that one was willing to give as well as display it. With an air of expecting a refusal, he then suggested his guest showed such a willingness by submitting to a further test. Hearing he was to hand over his wallet, to be taken away by the couple and brought back with the deeds and other documents pertaining to the sale, he had known there was only one course left open to him. If he refused, this would be seized upon as a reason to exclude him from the deal and any delay in the Pastor's arrival in Austin would be excused on the grounds of there having been no suitable Eastern Traditional Baptist available in Fort Worth to carry out the transaction. Telling himself the profit must be well worthwhile for his host to be willing to put in jeopardy an opportunity to take over a church in a wealthy neighborhood, he had acceded to the suggestion. Accepting the proffered wallet with obvious reluctance, the Pastor promised to tell the cashier he would settle the check when he and his daughter came back. Alice had offered to remain with Penfold, but her father had refused on the grounds that for her to do so would render the test of trust pointless.

Left to himself, the young man decided he would have another portion of the apple crumble that he had found so enjoyable. Adding it to the check his host would have to pay would do something to alleviate his annoyance over having been subjected to the second test. Glancing around for the waitress who had served at their table, he saw she was speaking with the cashier. Before he could try to attract her attention, she walked toward him.

"Excuse me, sir," the woman said, holding out a sheet of paper. "Could you settle the check now, please?"

"*Me?*" Penfold asked.

"Yes, sir," the waitress confirmed. "I'm going off duty now and need to have it cleared before I leave."

"That's no concern of mine!" Penfold stated. "The man I've been dining with said he'd settle the check when he came back."

"Is that what he told you, sir?"

"It is!"

"That's strange," the waitress claimed, glancing at the maître d'hôtel and making a motion with her head. "The gentleman told the cashier *you* would pay; and you waved to show it was all right with you."

"He said *what?*" the young man demanded, glaring across the room. The couple with whom he had dined had already left the café, so he went on, "But Pastor Salford told me he'd pay when he came back!"

"Is something wrong, Mrs. Blake?" the maître d'hôtel inquired, he and the cashier having converged on the table in response to the signal given by the waitress.

"This *gentleman* won't settle his check—!" the waitress began.

"It isn't *my* check to settle!" Penfold protested. "Pastor Salford said he'd arrange to settle it when he came back!"

"Well now, *sir,* I find that mighty *strange,*" drawled the big and burly cashier, exchanging a glance redolent of suspicion with the equally brawny maître d'. "You see, the reverend gentleman told me that *you* would wave to show how it'd be *you* who'd be paying when you was ready to leave."

"But that wasn't what he told *me!*" Penfold denied, with less than his usual bombast as he studied the polite and yet somehow menacing fashion in which the two men were regarding him. "He's going to the Cattlemen's Hotel to collect some papers, and he said he'd arrange with you to pay when he came back."

"Are you sure it's the *Cattlemen's Hotel* he's going to?" the maître d' inquired.

"Yes," Penfold confirmed.

"Correct me happen I'm wrong, will you, Mr. Beaumont?" requested the maître d', looking at his fellow employee. "But I seem to recollect as how the Cattlemen's Hotel is down to the left from here?"

"It was the last time I looked, Mr. Hoffman," the cashier replied.

"And yet the reverend gentleman and his lady turned *right* when they went out of the door," the maître d' asserted. "Do you reckon, them being strangers in town, they could have got themselves all turned around and lost?"

"You mean they haven't gone to the hotel?" Penfold yelped.

"If they have," the maître d' replied. "They're taking a roundabout way to it."

"I'll go and fetch them b—!" Penfold commenced and started to move forward, but the two burly men moved until effectively blocking his path.

"Now I'm not saying's how it's so in *your* case, *sir*," the maître d' interrupted, his manner still icily polite, while also implying he believed there was a possibility of the bill not being paid. "But I've heard that one *before*. Only then, none of them came back. Like I said, though, I'm not allowing that's what you've got in mind. Only, I reckon the best thing for all concerned would be for *you* to settle the check before you leave, then go and see the reverend gentleman about the *mistake*."

"But I let him take away my wall—!" Penfold began, conscious that everybody in the room was staring at him. Then a full realization of what he had allowed to happen struck him. At that moment, he felt the weight of something in the outside pocket of his jacket. Aware that the longer he stood arguing, the more time he was granting to the departed couple, he snatched out the wallet he had found in the hotel. Opening it, he snarled bitterly, "Tell me how much the check comes to and I'll pay it!"

19

You Can't Cheat an Honest Man

"That went off smoothly, 'Parson,' " Belle Starr remarked, as she and the elderly, somberly attired man who had claimed to be "Pastor Samuel Salford" were walking away from the Crystal Room Café.

"So it did, my dear, so it did," agreed Reginald Higgert, whose physical appearance and the religious pose he almost always employed when conducting a confidence trick had caused him to be given the sobriquet "Parson." Despite retaining something of its harsh timbre, his voice had become more amiable and even respectful. "I don't know about you, but I always find it most *satisfying* when I've taken down a thoroughly unpleasant mark like him."

"So do I," the lady outlaw admitted, thinking how vast was the difference between the apparently austere and forbidding exterior of her companion and his true nature. The rasp that never left his voice resulted from a vocal defect, although it was most useful in helping create the kind of character he most frequently adopted when engaged upon his chosen field of endeavor.

"Going by what I saw of him, he's the sort of Christian who always takes a shotgun to church so's he'll be sure to get whatever he's praying for. There's one thing I'll give *you*, though, Parson. I've never seen anybody who can touch you when it comes to picking the right mark."

"Now that, coming from *you*, my dear, is what I call a real *tribute*!" declared the leathery-faced con- juneero. Although a stranger would have noticed little or no change in his grim expression, he directed what Belle identified as a glance of delight her way and was clearly flattered by her compliment. "And I'm in your debt for helping me to pull it off. Blast it, if I've told Alice once, I've told her a dozen times that if she has to take up with a married man, she should make sure he doesn't have a jealous wife nearby who'll start pulling hair and have them all thrown into the pokey for disturbing the peace. Until I happened across you so fortuitously, I thought I would have to miss out on Penfold and my every instinct told me I'd not be likely to find anybody better in Fort Worth to set up for the old 'Proof of Trust' game."

"Shucks, I was only too happy to help you out," Belle asserted with sincerity, having learned almost everything she knew about organizing and running confidence tricks from the man at her side. Then, as she continued, her voice took on a slightly wistful note. "What brought me to Cowtown didn't pan out and I was at a loose end."

"I must confess I was surprised to find you here," Higgert drawled. "From what I'd heard, you had a team working the trail-end towns."

"I was and doing pretty well at it," the lady outlaw replied. "But I thought Kansas was going to become a little mite too hot for comfort."

There had been a not entirely unexpected repercus- sion as a result of the way in which Belle had taken her revenge upon David Icke. Unlike some better-publicized peace officers in Kansas, Town Marshal Kail Beauregard of Mulrooney was most competent and conscientious in the performance of his duties. Already wondering why the playwright had felt it necessary to employ an alias and to hire bodyguards, he had not considered the death of the three men as bringing the matter to an end. Instead, he had made a thorough investigation. In the course of it, he had learned much that the lady outlaw would have preferred to remain undiscovered. On hearing of his investigations, having the greatest respect for his ability, she had concluded a change of location—preferably far removed from his area of jurisdiction—was advisable. Having divided the not inconsiderable profits of their association with the other members of her team, she had told them to go their separate ways and promised to notify them when she was ready to resume operations.

Electing to travel southward alone, although Sammy Crane and Blue Duck were going in the same general direction, Belle had intended visiting her parents at their ranch in Oklahoma Territory. Learning there could be an earlier opportunity than she had anticipated for a meeting with the only man who had ever captured her heart and affections, she had revised her decision. Unfortunately, on arriving at Fort Worth and making inquiries, she had discovered Mark Counter was no longer in the vicinity.[1]

---

1. *How the romance between Belle Starr and Mark Counter commenced, developed, and was brought to an untimely end by her death is told in* Part One, "The Bounty On Belle Starr's Scalp," TROUBLED RANGE; *its "expansion,"* CALAMITY, MARK AND BELLE; RANGELAND HERCULES, THE BAD BUNCH; THE GENTLE GIANT; Part Two, "We Hang Horse Thieves High," J.T.'S HUNDREDTH; Part Four, "A Lady Known As Belle," THE HARD RIDERS, *and* GUNS IN THE NIGHT. *J.T.E.*

Due to her sojourn in the trail-end towns having proved so lucrative, although her hopes for a pleasant rendezvous with the handsome blond giant member of the OD Connected ranch's floating oufit had failed to materialize, the lady outlaw had not meant to indulge in any illegal activities in Fort Worth. However, having met Higgert at the home of a mutual friend and been informed of his dilemma, she had offered to play the role of his "downtrodden and browbeaten daughter" as a temporary replacement for his indisposed regular partner. Not only had she felt indebted to him for past favors, she had wanted to watch an acknowledged master of their illicit occupation in action.

As Belle was already aware, for almost every type of confidence trick to succeed, there must be a willingness on the part of the intended victim to take what appeared to be an unfair advantage of somebody else's misfortune or difficulties. While giving her instruction in such matters, Higgert had insisted there was much truth in the premise "You can't cheat a honest man."[2] As with the other advice she had received from him, experience had taught her the assumption was all too frequently correct. It certainly was in the case of Hubert Charles Penfold the Third.

Despite knowing how best they might make the acquaintance of their intended victim, the lady outlaw and the elderly conjuneero were equally aware that the need to make a hurried departure might arise. With this in mind, they had timed their arrival at the Cattlemen's Hotel on the previous day to be shortly before the clerk in charge of the reception desk was

---

2. *In addition to having frequently made such an assertion throughout his career, the late and great W.C. Fields also wrote the screenplay—under the psuedonym "Charles Bogle"—and starred in the 1939 movie,* YOU CAN'T CHEAT A HONEST MAN. *J.T.E.*

due to go off duty. Normally, if asked for accommodation by would-be guests who had no baggage, there would have been a request that payment in advance for at least one night was given as evidence of good faith. Taken in completely by the aura of religious respectability presented by the couple, the clerk had accepted without question the explanation that their trunks would be brought from the stagecoach depot as soon as the agent could arrange for delivery. Nor, being convinced he was dealing with a genuine member of the clergy, had he thought to inform his relief of the situation when handing over the desk prior to going home.

Regardless of his belief that Penfold had the requisite qualities to fall for the deception, Higgert had taken the precaution of conducting what he claimed to be an infallible test to ensure he was correct in his assumption. Having placed the wallet in the passage, he and Belle had kept watch from their room. Seeing the way in which the young man behaved on making the "find," the elderly conjuneero had declared this proved he was sufficiently lacking in scruples to be susceptible. By following him into the reception lobby, having made sure he had become aware of them as fellow guests the night before, they had avoided the suspicion that would almost certainly have been aroused if they had tried to make his acquaintance elsewhere.

Glancing at the lady outlaw as they were talking, the elderly conjuneero decided he could not fault the performance she had given during the main part of the swindle. The part she had been called upon to play, at short notice, was of importance in that it helped to create the required impression where the intended victim was concerned. Despite it having been the first time she had taken the role, he was willing to concede she had been at least as effective as

would his regular partner. Such was her histrionic
ability that, using only simple makeup and the unflattering clothing he had provided, she had been able to
prevent even the slightest suggestion of her true per-
sonality from showing. In fact, had he not known her,
he felt sure that he too would have accepted her as
what she was pretending to be.

Taking everything into account, Higgert felt considerable satisfaction over the way in which the beautiful young woman he regarded as something of a
protégé had turned out. Although their paths had
crossed several times over the years, after he had given
her lessons in the conducting of various confidence
tricks, they had not previously worked together. Having done so, he concluded that she had absorbed all
the advice he had passed on to her. What was more,
he decided she justified the claims regarding her
expertise that he had heard made by other members
of their very specialized illegal profession. He also
wished that, competent as she was, his regular partner
possessed an equal amount of talent.

"Unless I miss my guess, my dear," the conjuneero
remarked, the code of conduct by which he and his
companion lived preventing him from asking what
had made Kansas become "a little mite too hot for
comfort," "young Penfold is deciding to order something else and have it added to the check."

"I wouldn't want to bet against him doing it,"
Belle replied. "And I'd dearly love to see his piggy
little face when he finally gets around to realizing
that, not only are we not coming back, but he's
going to be stuck with paying for the meal. It's just a
pity he'll be able to use the money from your wallet
to do so."

"Rather him than me, my dear," Higgert declared,
with a frosty grin that gave an indication of his
far-from-somber and humorless true nature. "While

they will pass muster unless most closely scrutinized, those bills in the leather I put out for him to find weren't printed by the government of the good old U.S. of A."

"Do you think you were wise to dump 'queer jack' on him, Parson?" the lady outlaw inquired. "He's going to scream like a fattening shoat being knife-stuck for butchering when he finds out how he's been taken. It isn't likely the town marshal would call in the Rangers for a simple confidence game, he's not that important. But they're almost certain to be brought in when it comes out there's counterfeit money involved."

"That's true," the elderly conjuneero conceded, but showing no sign of finding the possibility of investigation by the Texas Rangers disturbing. For all that, he knew the reminder had been given with his interests at heart and not through fear of being involved personally, so he was grateful to his beautiful companion for her concern. Wanting to alleviate this, he continued, "However, I doubt whether anybody, unless sufficiently experienced in such matters and having reason to be on the lookout for them, would detect they aren't the real thing. By the time this is discovered, even if it should happen hereabouts, I'll long have shaken the dust of Fort Worth from my heels. In fact, my dear, I have fond expectations of making good my departure even before our friend back at the Crystal Room realizes he's been taken for a sucker."

"Are you going without Alice?" Belle wanted to know, satisfied there would be no immediate reper-cussions as a result of employing counterfeit money in the trick.

"We never travel together, at least not as 'father' and 'daughter,'" Higgert replied. "But, even if to do so would be *most* injudicious, I have no intention of leaving her to languish in durance vile. Annoying as some of her habits can be, saving only your good self, she's the best backup I've had in many a year. So I've made arrangements to secure her early release, left the necessary finances and instructions for where to join up with me. What're your plans, my dear?"

"There's nothing to hold me in Cowtown now, so I'm figuring to be on my way as soon as I've changed clothes. Like you always taught me, I don't stick around after I've helped pull a game."

"It's a good policy. But would it be indiscreet of me to inquire in which direction you'll be traveling?"

"Not at all," Belle answered. She knew her companion only wanted to avoid finding himself in a location where she was engaged upon some kind of confidence trick and perhaps, inadvertently, interfering with, or even spoiling, the scheme. "I haven't worked here in Texas for a fair spell and thought I'd drift down to Austin to find out whether it has anything to offer. Not that I'm thinking of starting back to work just yet, unless something good comes up that I can handle lone handed. My team have scattered and will want to do some spending before we get together again. So, after I've looked things over around Austin, I'm figuring on visiting with my folks for a spell of peace and quiet."

"Give them my felicitations when you get there," requested the elderly conjuneero. "And tell them I'll be dropping by the next time I'm in the Indian Nations."

"I'll do th—!" the lady outlaw commenced, but there was an interruption before she could finish what she was saying.

"Turn around slow and easy, with both hands showing empty!" commanded a harsh voice with a Chicago accent from behind the couple.

20

SHE ISN'T THE ONE

Hearing what was clearly an order directed at them, Belle Starr and Reginald "Parson" Higgert were brought back to a conscious awareness of their surroundings. Discovering the nature of the location they had reached while engaged in their conversation, they came immediately to a stop. A quick exchange of glances informed each that the other did not know who was addressing them. However, both were equally certain of one thing. No friend who had penetrated their disguise, even if otherwise given to practical joking, would have spoken in such a fashion. Realizing that the speaker was unlikely to have failed to take the precaution of having the means to back up the threatening words, they concluded it would be advisable to comply. Having ascertained who and what they were up against, they could decide how best to deal with the unexpected situation.

The maître d' hôtel had not made a mistake when telling Hubert Charles Penfold the Third in which direction the lady outlaw and the elderly conjuneero had turned on leaving the Crystal Room Café.

On checking into the Cattlemen's Hotel the previous day, having told Belle that attempting such an economy always brought him luck, Higgert had deliberately sought to avoid having to pay in advance for the room they would be occupying overnight. Although he would have had a couple of suitably weighted old trunks delivered, should the matter of baggage been raised later, the timing of their arrival had allowed them to obtain admittance with only such of their belongings as could be carried upon their persons. Therefore, when taking Penfold for the lunch that was the prelude to springing their trap upon him, they had had no intention of returning. Because neither had left anything behind that needed to be collected, having served their purpose by presenting them with an apparently innocent reason for making the acquaintance of their proposed victim, there was no reason for them to go back.

Having brought the confidence trick to its successful conclusion, Belle and Higgert were making their way to the home of the mutual friend at which they had met the day before. Once there, each would make changes to clothing and appearances ready to leave Forth Worth.

While talking, the lady outlaw and her companion had been walking in an apparently unhurried fashion away from the business section. Confident that it would be some time before Penfold realized he had been tricked, they had sought to avoid doing anything that might draw unwanted attention to them. Aware that an alert peace officer who saw them behaving in such a fashion might become suspicious, they had refrained from looking behind them. Even when turning from the street, to pass along an alley between two stores that had already closed for the day, they had not heard anything to suggest they were being followed.

The first indication of possible danger had come with the command to stop!

Following her usual habit, unless wearing its un-modified mate in the fast-draw holster of her gunbelt, Belle was carrying her short-barreled Manhattan Navy Model revolver in the bulky black reticule her left hand was grasping. However, she made no attempt to reach for it with the right as she began to turn. Nor, although she knew he had weapons concealed upon his person, did the elderly conjuneero try to arm him-self. Being equally cognizant of the danger such an action would create if performed prematurely, he too did nothing more than carry out the instructions they had been given.

Running her gaze quickly over the men who were approaching along the alley, the lady outlaw decided she was not acquainted in any way with either. A quick look at Higgert told her, without the need for words, that he too did not know them. Returning her attention to them, she concluded it was the one at the left who had spoken. Just over middle height, bulky and hard-looking, his features were sallow and heavily mustached. Despite wearing clothes indicative of city living, he held a Merwin & Hulbert Army Pocket revolver with an air of being sufficiently competent to prove dangerous at such close quarters. If no longer in the peak of physical condition, the second man was taller and well-built. He too was dressed after the fashion of a town dweller, but more fashionably and expensively. Exuding a suggestion of comradely bon-homie frequently cultivated by one class of politician, he did not appear to be armed in any way.

"If robbery under arms is your intention, brothers," Higgert boomed, reverting to his sternly religious demeanor, but making sure he kept both hands clear of his sides, "you've chosen badly. I'm but a poor servant of the Good Lord and—!"

"Damned if you ain't good's I've allus heard, Parson!" interrupted the man with the revolver, confirming Belle's assumption that he had delivered the orders. "If I didn't know better, you'd take me in the same's you've done to plenty of suckers."

"Just a moment, Mr. Steeples!" the second man put in, having given all his attention to the lady outlaw. He had a Southern drawl, with the timbre of one long used to public speaking. "You've made a mistake!"

"How do you mean?" the armed man demanded, neither relaxing his vigilance nor offering to lower his short-barreled revolver.

"You promised to catch the woman who swindled me in Dallas," the Southron reminded, and waved a hand toward Belle. "And this isn't her!"

"It was a Belle Starr's took you," the armed man asserted. "And here she is!"

"She *may* be Belle Starr," the Southron replied, still studying the lady outlaw and paying no attention to Higgert. Although far from flattering in one respect, his all-too-obvious disbelief was also a tribute to her powers of disguise. "But—!"

"She's Belle Starr for sure!" the armed man declared, and gestured with his revolver toward the conjuneero. "I got word's how this old bastard'd asked her to side him 'cause his own gal'd got throwed in the pokey. So this's her."

"That's as may be," the other man answered. "But I don't care whether she's Belle Starr or not. She isn't the one who swindled me."

"Are you sure?" the Chicagoan demanded.

"Of course I'm *sure*!" the Southron stated, his manner suggesting he was not used to having his words questioned. "Damn it all, man, don't you think

I'd recognize the woman who took me for two thousand five hundred dollars?" He did not wait for a reply, but continued just as heatedly. "Well, she isn't the one!"

"Then it looks like you lose out," the armed man commented. "But not *me*. There's dodgers on both of them. Top of that, they've likely just took some poor sucker's'll be willing to pay up for getting his money back.".

While the pair were talking, Belle had been surveying the situation and thinking fast. The name given to the man with the revolver had struck a responsive chord in her memory. Their paths had not crossed, but she had heard him mentioned more than once during her recently ended sojourn in Kansas. Along with his brothers, Albert "High" and Wilfred "Little," Joseph "Church" Steeples had begun to acquire a reputation as a competent bounty hunter since coming west from Chicago. According to the accounts that had reached her, if falling short of the standards reached by many range country–trained gunfighters, he was sufficiently skillful to pose a very serious threat under the circumstances. Certainly, he was not a man with whom it would pay to take chances.

Hearing the reference to "dodgers on both of them," the lady outlaw swung a look at her companion. His gaze was turned her way and, having given a shake of his head, he mouthed the words "On you?," to which she gave a negative response. To the best of her knowledge, because she always selected victims who would be disinclined to report their losses to the authorities, no law-enforcement agency had put out wanted posters offering a reward for her capture.

Yet, taking into account that Steeples had been operating in Kansas, Belle realized there was a possibility of a bounty on her. If Town Marshal Kail Beauregard had discovered her connection with David Icke, he might have circularized other law-enforcement agencies without her having heard of it. Even if this was not the case, however, she had no desire to be handed over to the local peace officers. Nor, she felt sure, had Higgert. If this happened, Penfold could supply all the evidence needed to make a case against them.

Regardless of being convinced that her companion had an equal wish to escape, the lady outlaw knew any attempt would be fraught with danger. They were faced by a man who, unless rumor lied, would not hesitate to use his gun if given provocation. What was more, ostensibly a law-abiding citizen dealing with criminals, he could open fire without needing to worry about legal consequences. The same did not apply to them, if either should shoot him. Therefore, their only hope of escaping was to render him *hors de combat* without killing. However, unless they were able to create a diversion and distract him, at least one of them was certain to take lead should they try to do so.

Belle did not realize it, but she was in grave danger!

While no law-enforcement agency had put a bounty on her, Steeples knew he could collect money for killing her!

When contacted by Armond Chauvelin, who was seeking vengeance after having learned the true identity of "Senora Donna Maria Constanza de la Santa Rosa," the Steeples brothers had known the risks they would face if they were successful in the proposition he made to them. These had increased, they realized, when their search for the lady outlaw had led them to Texas.

As far as the brothers had been able to ascertain, despite her participation in numerous lucrative confidence tricks, there were no outstanding warrants for the arrest of their intended victim. On the other

hand, her close association with members of Ole
Devil Hardin's floating outfit in particular meant she
could not be dealt with as if she were an ordinary
wanted outlaw. If they wished to avoid bringing those
deadly efficient young Texans down upon them, it
was imperative that she was killed in what would
have the appearance of self-defense while resisting a
citizen's arrest.

Having separated from his brothers, who were following up other leads, Church Steeples had seen the
opportunity of seeking the excuse he required, and
also a witness to substantiate his story of what happened. Learning that a prominent local politician had
fallen victim to a confidence trick perpetrated by a
beautiful woman, he had offered his services. Blaming
Belle Starr, who he had discovered was making for
Fort Worth, he had persuaded Owen O'Brien to
accompany him so as to recover the money. Searching
for her, having been told she was helping Higgert,
he and O'Brien had seen them leaving the Crystal
Room Café. Following them until they had left the
sight of the few people on the street, he had drawn his
revolver and forced them to a halt.

Now Steeples was waiting for anything that
would offer him an excuse to start shooting, with his
companion—a man of some importance in the area—
available to support his claim to have acted in self-
defense against two known criminals.

Before the bounty hunter could say or do anything
to bring about the response he required, there was an
interruption!

Having discovered he had been tricked, much
sooner than was anticipated by Belle and Higgert,
Penfold had settled the check and was preparing to
leave the café. At the sight of them walking along the
street, his first impulse had been to shout for assistance. However, failing to locate a peace officer in the

immediate vicinity, he had realized that to do so would put them to flight. Satisfied he could deal personally with the old man and expecting no trouble from the "daughter," he had set off in pursuit. Although he had noticed the two men following his quarry into the alley, his only thought was that they would be available to help him make the capture. On reaching it, being unable to see the revolver held by Steeples, he failed to attach any significance to the way in which the group were standing.

"Got y—!" the red-faced young man yelped, rushing into the alley.

"Get him, Hank!" Belle yelled, startled by the sight of the victim she had believed would still be awaiting the return of her "father," but having the presence of mind to try to take advantage of the unexpected development.

At the sound of the voice and footsteps behind him, Steeples glanced over his shoulder. Seeing the clearly angry figure approaching, he reached the conclusion that the lady outlaw had hoped to produce, and, spitting an obscenity, he began to swing around. Also deceived by her words, Penfold threw himself forward with his hands reaching for the revolver being turned his way.

The instant Steeples was distracted, Belle and Higgert made the most of the opportunity her quick wits had created!

Although the conjuneero had a Remington Double Derringer in an easily accessible concealment holster, he did not wish to indulge in gunplay and he considered something less noisy would serve his purpose. Displaying a surprising speed for one of his age, he shook his wrist and stepped forward. Released from its holder strapped to his right wrist, a leather-wrapped and spring-loaded sap slipped from his sleeve into the waiting hand. Swinging it around almost horizontally, he aimed under the curly brim of the derby hat, which would have reduced the effect of a blow to the top of the head. Struck at the base of the skull, Steeples crumpled like a punctured balloon. He had begun to squeeze the trigger of his double-action revolver, but the hammer was not yet far enough back to operate and it fell from his grasp unfired.

Almost within reaching distance, Penfold was unable to halt as the man he was intending to tackle started to collapse. Instead, he threw his arms around Steeples. The weight of the unconscious bounty hunter caused him to lose his balance. Before he could even try to regain it, Higgert's left hand knocked the hat from his head and the right delivered a blow with the sap that toppled him and his burden to the ground.

"Stand still and keep quiet, mister!" Belle commanded, bringing the Manhattan out of her reticule while her companion was arming himself. Seeing he needed no help from her, she devoted her attention to the Southron. "You and I don't have any quarrel, going by what you said, so I don't want to have to hurt you."

"We're in agreement on that, young lady," O'Brien replied. "No offense intended, but are you really Belle Starr?"

"I am," the lady outlaw confirmed. "Did the woman who swindled you claim she was?"

"No," the Southron answered. "That was Steeples's idea. When he came to see me he said it must be you who did it, and offered to help me find you and get my money back."

"That's the oldest game in the book," Belle stated. "Anyways, my friend and I are going now. I'd sooner we didn't have to put you down like those two, so will you give us your word as a Southern gentleman not to raise an alarm for five minutes?"

"I will," the Southron promised immediately, having no desire to be struck down and confident this would happen if he did otherwise. Then his instincts as a politician took over and he went on, "By the way, Miss Starr, the next time you meet Captain Fog, or Mark Counter, tell them Owen O'Brien of Dallas sends his best wishes."

"Count on me to do just that," the lady outlaw replied, aware of what else was implied by the request. "Let's go, Parson. We can count on Mr. O'Brien to keep his word."

"And I'll make sure the local officers know it wasn't *you* who took me in, Miss Starr," the politician offered, feeling sure his behavior would be mentioned to the two young men he had named and, hopefully, bring him the good offices of their influential family connections. "Goodbye. I won't do anything for five minutes, unless you need longer—!"

"Five minutes will be fine!" Belle declared. "*Adios,* Mr. O'Brien. I hope you find that woman and get your money back."

"You wouldn't be interested in finding her for me, I don't suppose?" hinted the politician.

"Bounty hunting isn't my style," the lady outlaw refused, despite wondering which female conjuneero had performed the swindle. "As long as she doesn't try to put the blame on me by using my name, I've got no quarrel with her."

"It was just a thought," O'Brien sighed, feeling sure the beautiful young woman could have found her fellow confidence trickster if she wished. "Goodbye, then, Miss Starr, sir. May you both get away safely."

21

LET'S HAVE ANOTHER DRINK

"Blast it, we're too late!" Belle Starr exclaimed, acting as if she had expected a response to the tug she had given upon the bell cord hanging down from a corner of the expensively furnished sitting room in the mansion to which she had brought an intended victim. "Aunt Selena-Mae's servants have already left for their night off!"

For once, while engaged upon an illicit activity, the lady outlaw was not making use of a wig. Such an aid to altering her appearance was not needed for the character she had created. Despite being without a hat of any kind, the shortness of her brunette hair, taken with the severe lines of her plain blue blouse and black skirt, was helping to give credence to the part she was playing.

Having carried out her departure from Fort Worth without further difficulty, Belle had not taken the shortest route to Austin. Instead, she had made her way from one gathering place for outlaws to another, so as to renew acquaintanceships and get to know the current state of affairs with regard to criminal activities in Texas. Out of curiosity, she had tried to learn the identity of the female confidence trickster who had swindled Owen O'Brien. For once, her efforts had come to nothing. Nobody would admit to knowledge of the woman, nor of having heard complaints from other victims.

Regardless of the failure to gain the information she sought, the lady outlaw considered traveling by such an indirect trail had brought more than one benefit. The most important, to her way of thinking, was the discovery that Armond Chauvelin had persuaded the Steeples brothers to seek her out and take revenge for the trick she had played upon him and his wife. However, as far as she had been able to ascertain, the trio had lost track of her after she had fled from Forth Worth. Nevertheless, doubting whether they would give up the chase, she had been extra alert while continuing her journey to the state capitol.

On reaching Austin, particularly in consideration of there being hunters looking for her, Belle had concluded she could hardly have selected a better time for a visit. A gathering of adherents for the cause of women's suffrage was taking place, which meant she would be less likely to attract attention as a stranger than on almost any other occasion she might have chosen. Having heard of the suffragette meeting while on the way and appreciating how she might turn it to her advantage, she had brought along suitable attire from one of the numerous caches of clothing and other equipment left in the care of trusted friends.

Staying at an otherwise respectable boardinghouse, owned by a maternal maiden aunt—whose favorite niece she was and who took pleasure in helping her nefarious activities—the lady outlaw employed a different character while on the premises. Using a blond wig drawn into a bun, buckteeth and a large false nose, she gave the impression of being an unattractive, newly hired, Swedish housemaid. Away from her hiding place, however, she dressed, looked, and behaved in a fashion that allowed her to mingle with, and pass as, one of the feminist visitors.

Despite Belle being in agreement that members of her sex should have the right to vote in political elections, even though her criminal activities precluded her from being able to do so, she had quickly found herself forming a dislike for the majority of those who had congregated to advocate suffrage. Watching and listening to the antics of the well-to-do feminists of "liberal" pretensions, she had considered their attitude and behavior was doing much to alienate many people, women as well as men, who might otherwise have given support to the issue. Such was her nature that her animosity had produced a desire to prey upon those responsible for having aroused it.

Studying the feminists, the lady outlaw had selected the one she considered to be the most deserving of her attentions.

Matching Belle in height and, as far as could be discerned due to the almost masculine cut and style of her clothing, with an equally curvaceous figure, the Honorable Drusilla St. John-Belleweather—the first part of the hyphenated name apparently being pronounced "Sinjun"—was obviously born into the British upper class. Like many of her background on both sides of the Atlantic Ocean who openly professed "liberal" persuasions, she was arrogant and overbearing in her treatment of anybody she regarded as a social inferior. The main topic of her conversation, invariably conducted in a loud voice, was the assertion that she was the equal of any man in most fields of endeavor. Learning this belief extended to gambling, the lady outlaw had concluded it offered a way in which she could be trapped, and Belle had made the necessary arrangements to do so.

Waiting until hearing the Englishwoman complain about having been refused admittance to an exclusive social club noted for its games of chance for high stakes, Belle had made her acquaintance by claiming that she also had been thwarted in a desire to enter and participate.[1] Introducing herself as "Sylvia Montane of New Orleans," the lady outlaw had claimed there was a group of the feminist visitors who shared their willingness to gamble and were going to gather at the mansion owned by her aunt to play poker. Invited to sit in, the aristocratic feminist had agreed and Belle had arranged for them to go together. She had said they would be the first to arrive, as the family were on vacation and she wanted to make sure everything was ready before the other players arrived.

Like the Chauvelins in Newton, Kansas, Belle had been fortunate enough to obtain a location suitable for her purpose. Having learned he was in Austin while traveling from Fort Worth, she had contacted a dishonest butler with whom she had done business elsewhere. The owners of a neighboring mansion had closed it while taking a trip. To save money, they had given their staff a vacation and arranged with the butler to have him keep an eye on the property. In return for a share of the profits, the butler had promised to give her access and leave everything ready on the night she requested.

Arriving with the Englishwoman in a cab operated

---

1. *Although at the period of this narrative gambling for high stakes was still considered a masculine occupation, a few women—"Poker Alice" and "Madame Mustache" being the most prominent—had gained acceptance and were highly respected as players. Both ladies make "guest" appearances in* Part Two, "The Gamblers," THE WILD-CATS, *and* THE HIDE AND HORN SALOON. *J.T.E.*

by another acquaintance, the lady outlaw had found everything was as she had instructed. Although the rest of the mansion was in darkness, the sitting room was illuminated and a door that gave access to it without needing to use the main entrance was unlocked. During the drive, to lessen the chance of the deserted aspect of the building arousing suspicion, she had explained that her aunt would not approve and, hoping to prevent the servants from reporting she had held the game on the premises, had told them to take the night off.

"One can always rely upon the hired help to take advantage of one, if they're given half a chance," Drusilla stated, clearly having accepted the reason she had been given. Although she was beautiful, it was marred by the way in which her honey-blond hair was drawn into a tight bun, and by the monocle she invariably wore, emphasizing the arrogance of her demeanor. Apart from wearing a white "boater" hat, her attire was much the same as that of Belle. Glancing around disdainfully while removing the headdress and placing it on the table, she went on, "I shudder to think of what that maid of mine might be up to while I'm not there to keep an eye on her. Nice place you folks have, old gel. It *almost* comes up to *our* standards."

"Why, thank you, *darling*," the lady outlaw replied with well-simulated, apparently thinly veiled, annoyance, deciding it would be especially satisfying to teach the other the costly lesson she intended. Leading the way to the table in the center of the room and indicating the glasses and decanters on the sidepiece, she went on, "Do have a seat and let me fetch you a drink."

"I'll take a port, if there is any," the Englishwoman assented, drawing out a chair and sitting down, her attitude implying she considered the possibility unlikely.

"I hope this is to your liking," Belle commented,

having collected two glasses of the port she had asked
the butler to include in the decanters, knowing such
to be the other's usual drink. Reaching for the
reticule she had placed on the table and which was as
large as, if more stylish than, the one she used when
wearing poorer garb, she said, "I've brought the
cards—"

"Just a tick, old thing!" Drusilla interrupted, more
in the manner of an order than a request, setting
down the glass at which she had sipped as if expecting
the contents to be below her usual standard. "No
offense meant and all that sort of jolly rot, but you
know how *superstitious* we gamblers are. I always
seem to have the most *terrible* luck when I'm playing
with anybody else's cards, so would you mind most
awfully if we use the pack *I've* brought?"

"Have it your own way," Belle answered, watching
the Englishwoman reaching into a reticule almost the
same size as her own. She had had no intention of
relying upon cards prepared in advance, but added,
"I'm superstitious too and always find it's lucky for
me to open whatever deck I'll be using."

"Go ahead," Drusilla authorized, showing no hesitation before speaking.

Wondering if there might be more than just superstition behind the request, the lady outlaw accepted
the correctly sealed packet offered by the Englishwoman and subjected it to a quick yet careful examina-
tion. It was the product of a well-known and reputable
manufacturer, but she was aware that there were ways
to open, then close, the wrappings after the contents
had been marked or otherwise treated for cheating
purposes. Having been taught what to look for, by a
professional gambler skilled in such matters, she could
not detect anything to suggest this had happened.

Breaking open the seal, Belle extracted the deck
and tossed aside the jokers. Then she subjected the

cards to what appeared to be nothing more than a casual rippling under her right thumb. In reality, regardless of her assumptions about the packet, she was conducting a most effective test that would expose any secret markings there might be on the backs.[2] Satisfied there were none, she took the precaution of studying her intended victim to check for signs that other forms of cheating were contemplated. Everything seemed to be all right. Drusilla was not wearing any rings that could conceal a mirror, allowing the value of the cards to be discovered as they were being dealt, nor were her fingernails long or sharp enough to make marks on the backs during play. The tightness of the dark green blouse's cuffs precluded the use of a "hideout," or even concealing cards up the sleeve. All in all, it seemed the suggestion of using her own cards was nothing more than a precaution against being cheated, or mere genuine superstition.

"When are the rest of the gels coming?" the Englishwoman inquired, as the lady outlaw placed the cards on the table and sat down.

"They said they'd be along about eight-thirty," Belle replied, glancing at the grandfather clock in a corner of the room. "But you know what they're like when they get talking politics."

"I do."

"Would you care for another drink while we're waiting?"

"No, thank you. But what say you and I have a few hands to pass the time until they get here?"

"Let's do just that," Belle agreed, having meant to make the suggestion. "Straight draw, no wild cards,

---

2. *A detailed description of the kind of test conducted by Belle Starr is given in* Chapter Five, I'm Counting On You Losing, THE HIDE AND HORN SALOON. *J.T.E.*

and for table stakes, unless you've something else in mind?"

"I never play any other way," Drusilla claimed, and opened her reticule to take out a thick wad of money. "There's two thousand of your dollar-things here, old sport. Hope you and the others can match it?"

"I certainly can," the lady outlaw declared, having brought a similar sum and removing it from the bag she had placed to the right of where she was seated. "Shall we cut for deal?"

With the game commenced, Belle needed only a few hands to realize she was dealing with a most competent opponent. Judging by various indications, the Englishwoman was well-versed in more than just the playing tactics. However, the lady outlaw was unable to detect any attempts at employing cheating techniques to improve the run of the cards. Nor, due to the clearly knowledgeable scrutiny to which she was subjected, was she able to do so when dealing.

"Great heavens, just look at the time!" Drusilla exclaimed, after something over an hour of very competitive play had passed without any decisive advantage either way. "Where can those blasted gels be?"

"They should be here by now," Belle lied, then stretched. "I don't know about you, but my throat is dry. Let's have another drink, shall we?"

"I was hoping you'd ask," the Englishwoman declared. "That's quite an *adequate* port for over here."

Crossing to the sidepiece, the lady outlaw reached into a concealed pocket at the front of her skirt's waistband. Despite carrying the means to do so, it had not been her intention to resort to the measures she was contemplating. Nor would she have done so if the butler had not assured her he could evade any suggestion of complicity should her victim lodge a complaint with the town marshal. However, she concluded that she could not continue the pretense of there being other players coming for much longer and had decided to take the easy way out.

Extracting a small pillbox containing the kind of drug she had used on David Icke at Mulrooney, Belle tipped some into Drusilla's glass and added a measure of port. A quick shake speeded the dissolving process and removed all visible traces of the addition before she was ready to return. With this done, topping up her own glass, she picked up the tray from which she had served the first drinks and walked back to the table. Taking the glasses from it, the Englishwoman moved both in circular motions before setting them down.

"That's how my pater said the best bouquet could be given to port, old thing," Drusilla remarked, placing the correct glass in front of the lady outlaw. Raising her own in the manner of proposing a toast, she continued, "Here's strength to women's suffrage!"

"May it soon be coming!" Belle countered, remaining on her feet and tipping all the port down her throat as an inducement for the Englishwoman to do the same.

Aware of how quickly the potion could take effect, the lady outlaw knew she would not have long to wait after Drusilla duplicated her action by swallowing the contents of the glass. However, as she saw the other becoming aware that something was wrong and trying to rise, a wave of dizziness assailed her. Even as a realization of what must be causing it came to her, her legs buckled beneath her.

With almost simultaneous thuds, the two beautiful women collapsed and sprawled unconscious upon the floor.

22

GREAT MINDS THINK ALIKE

Although Belle Starr was not aware of it, on regaining consciousness some ninety minutes after falling to the floor, the sensations that assailed her were much the same as those experienced by David Icke when he recovered from having been drugged by her.

Several seconds elapsed before the lady outlaw was able to realize that she was not alone in her suffering!

Hearing a low groan from somewhere nearby, Belle forced herself to make the effort and raised her head from the carpet to investigate. What she saw indicated she was incorrect in her assumption that, by some inexplicable accident, she had caused herself to drink the drugged port prepared for her intended victim.

Looking far from arrogant, with the monocle dangling from her neck by its cord instead of at her left eye, the honey-blond Englishwoman was slowly struggling into a kneeling position. Finding she was under observation by the cause of her misfortunes, she let out a furious hiss and began to rise. Seeing the anger that came to her beautiful and patrician features, the lady outlaw concluded it was advisable to do likewise. Swaying as they came to their feet, each waited for the dizziness caused by her movements to clear away.

"Drug me, would you?" Drusilla St. John-Belleweather exclaimed as her stance steadied, stepping forward and swinging around her left hand an instant before Belle was ready to move.

Despite having so recently regained her faculties, the way in which the punch was delivered by the Englishwoman was indicative of considerable skill. In fact, struck on the side of the jaw, the lady outlaw might have counted herself fortunate that her assailant had not yet completely thrown off the effects of the potion she had administered. Even with such a disadvantage, she was sent by the impact in a twirling sprawl against the table. Brought to a halt, the pain caused by the blow cleared her head. However, although within reaching distance of her reticule, she made no attempt to draw out her Manhattan Navy Model revolver.

Glancing over her shoulder, Belle was spurred into motion by the sight of the honey blonde rushing forward. Wavering slightly as she thrust herself erect, she used the impetus of her turn to change the advance into a hurried involuntary retreat with an equally skillful punch by her clenched right fist. Despite the success she achieved, she did not believe the affair was over. Nevertheless, she continued to ignore the readily available weapon. Instead of arming herself, she set about acquiring a greater freedom of movement than would be possible while dressed in such a comparatively restrictive fashion.

As was the case with most of the clothing owned by the lady outlaw, the garments she was wearing had been made to help cope with the kind of situation she was now in. Hooking her thumbs into the waistband of her skirt, she gave a twisting tug that caused it to open. Allowing the garment to fall to the floor, leaving her clad below the blouse in black tights of the kind worn by certain types of female entertainers, and high button shoes, she stepped clear of it. However, even while doing so, she discovered that the advantage she had hoped to gain by discarding it might be nullified.

Having been sent reeling until reaching the wall by the sidepiece, the Englishwoman had clearly arrived at the same conclusions as the lady outlaw. What was more, although such a way of tailoring was far from common—in fact, Belle knew of only one other person who always had it done—the skirt worn by Drusilla was capable of just as speedy a removal. Regardless of the close-to-masculine lines of her outer attire, discarding it brought into view attire that was indisputably feminine. Not only were the red satin drawers trimmed with black lace, much briefer and far less decorous than might be expected from external appearances, the sheer black silk stockings and their fancy red suspender straps were in no way complimentary to the low-heeled and less-than-stylish shoes on her feet.

Surprised by finding out that the Englishwoman was able to escape from the skirt as easily as she had done, there was no time for the lady outlaw to wonder whether she too had come by the idea as a result of having made the acquaintance of Belle Boyd. It had been from the Rebel Spy, now serving as an agent for the United States Secret Service,[1] that Belle Starr had learned the secret of the readily opening waistband now fitted to all her garments.

---

1. *How the first meeting between Belle Starr and Bell "the Rebel Spy" Boyd came about is told in* THE BAD BUNCH, *and another occasion is described in* THE QUEST FOR BOWIE's BLADE. *Other "guest" and "starring" appearances by the latter are listed in* Footnote 8, APPENDIX TWO. *J.T.E.*

Freed from whatever restraints to mobility the discarded skirts would otherwise have imposed, the two beautiful women moved forward to resume hostilities!

In spite of bringing up their hands clenched in a manner indicating they had a knowledge of fistfighting, the pair did not indulge in any preliminary sparring. As soon as they judged they were in range, each began to throw punches. Being so evenly matched in size, the first blows arrived almost simultaneously. Caught on the cheek as her right hand arrived against Drusilla's left eye, Belle immediately sent her other knuckles up to the breast and received an equally solid hook to the solar plexus in return.

For several seconds, the toe-to-toe slugging went on with reckless abandon. However, combined with neither being at her best, the speed with which the pair sought to deliver their punches prevented either from producing one blow capable of rendering the recipient *hors de combat*. However, the exchange kept them at arm's length until a miss by Belle brought them together.

On going into something resembling a boxer's clinch, the combatants grappled. After giving and taking a couple of blows at close quarters, the lady outlaw learned her opponent's ability was not restricted to fistfighting. Feeling herself being grasped in a familiar way, she was unable to avoid a throw over Drusilla's hip. The thickness of the carpet cushioned her landing somewhat. Seeing the Englishwoman looming over her with a foot raised to stamp, she caught and twisted at it before it could descend. Sent staggering by the push she received, Drusilla was prevented from going down by colliding with the table. On turning away from it, she found Belle was already standing up.

Coming together, the lady outlaw and the Englishwoman continued to employ tactics more usual between men. Fists flew, wrestling holds were obtained and broken, throws of various kind sent first one and then the other flying. Somewhere along the way, without any deliberate intent, the right sleeve was torn from Belle's blouse. Later, her attempt to strangle Drusilla came to nothing when the cord of the monocle that she was using snapped. The punch that came up beneath her chin as the force she had been exerting caused her arms to open sent her stumbling backward.

Bending at the waist, the Englishwoman charged to ram her head into the lady outlaw's chest. Despite the croak of pain she elicited, the attack proved less beneficial than she wished. Driven backward and going down, Belle managed to grab and drag her assailant with her. Feeling her equilibrium being destroyed, Drusilla could not regain it. Forced to follow the other woman, the two knees that came up flipped her in a half-somersault to land on her back beyond the short-cropped brunette head.

Coming to their feet more slowly than they had earlier in the struggle, the embattled pair plunged together without hesitation. After trading a couple of less effective punches, they stumbled into each other's arms. Having struggled for a few seconds, they tripped and fell still locked in the mutually encircling limbs. Nor, despite the landing provoking gasps from both, did alighting on the carpet cause them to break away. Instead, they began to churn over and over in a tight, squirming mill.

Although both women had relied upon not inconsiderable skill at boxing and wrestling until falling, there was nothing scientific about the conflict that ensued. A growing exhaustion, mingled with primeval instincts for self-preservation, caused them to forget such basically masculine tactics and the fighting became entirely feminine in what was being done.

Hair was pulled, causing the destruction of the hitherto untouched honey-blond bun, or used as an aid to bang heads on the floor. Hands punched, slapped, grabbed, clutched, or scrabbled indiscriminately at faces, shoulders, backs, and bosoms. However, although attempts were made to scratch, neither had nails sufficiently long for them to break the skin. Shapely legs, stockings and tights soon ruined, flailed and intertwined incessantly. Knees were driven between thighs, or against stomachs, with an equally unguided vigor. Provoked by anger and mutual suffering, squeals, grunts, gasps, and garbled profanity served to punctuate the various instinctive activities.

The thrashing about on the carpet continued unabated for several minutes, taking the furiously struggling pair under the table and from one side to the other three times. Despite each having tried repeatedly, neither had been able to retain an ascendancy gained more than briefly before having it wrested from her. Then, without either having sought consciously to do so, they came to their knees and their fingers were interlocked. Sucking in gasping breaths, they engaged in a test of strength that brought them to their feet. Practically identical in physical attributes, their powers were equally sapped by previous exertion and they were in a state of stalemate. Realizing this at the same instant, they snatched apart their hands. Then, as if acting upon a prearranged signal, each put all she had into delivering a right cross.

As had happened with the first blows struck after the discarding of the skirts, the fists arrived almost simultaneously!

Driven across the room with no control over her movements, Belle went down by an easy chair.

Propelled in the opposite direction, buckling legs carrying her without conscious guidance, Drusilla sprawled across and slid from the table. Although neither was rendered unconscious, they were too far gone in exhaustion to have any thought of resuming the fight.

Some ten minutes went by before Belle was able to give any consideration to her position. With a return of cogent thought, she glanced over her shoulder while using the arm and seat of the chair to help her rise. Although the blood from her nose had dried up, she ached from head to toe. However, she realized her condition might have been far worse. It was obvious why the Englishwoman had not come to finish her off. With her hair resembling a well-soaked mop, left cheek discolored by a bruise, and the remnants of her ruined blouse flapping about her torso, Drusilla was only just hauling herself painfully from the floor with the arm of the chair she had occupied while playing poker.

"W—wait!" the honey blonde gasped, seeing the lady outlaw turning toward her.

"H—had enough?" Belle inquired, just as breathlessly, hoping the answer would be in the affirmative.

"From the way you look and I feel," Drusilla estimated, but there was no longer any trace in her voice of the arrogant bombast that had so annoyed the lady outlaw ever since their first meeting. "We *both* have had enough."

"You could be right at that," Belle conceded, subsiding in a tired slump onto the easy chair. "I'll admit I've felt more *lively* in my time."

"You know, old thing, now you *mention* it, so have I," seconded the honey blonde, also sitting down. "Blast it, I must be getting *old*."

"If you are, honey," the lady outlaw drawled, feeling no concern over her former antagonist, being so close to the Manhattan Navy revolver in her reticule, "I'd hate to have tangled with you when you were young and spry."

"But I *must* be!" Drusilla insisted. "I really believed you were one of those dreadful *women*-women who're infesting the hotel. You were acting so obnoxiously, I thought you deserved to have your corns trimmed."

"You didn't do so badly in that yourself," Belle confessed. "I had you figured along those lines myself."

"I can't remember you making a single slip that might have warned me off," the Englishwoman asserted with sincerity. "It wasn't until I felt my head starting to go whoozy and guessed you'd slipped something nasty into the port that I realized something *might* be wrong."

"Seeing the room starting to spin around was what started me to get just a teensy mite *suspicious* about you," the lady outlaw admitted, deciding the honey blonde had a sense of humor much like her own. "Until then, you hadn't done a thing to make me change my mind about you. I just kept right on thinking you were an unpleasant Limey soft-shell, but you knew too much about cards for me to chance cheating. So, when you seemed to be starting to wonder why the rest of the players hadn't shown up, I decided to slip you a mickey and get it over."

"Which just goes to prove mater was right when she said, 'Great minds think alike,' " Drusilla asserted, as if imparting information of great importance and, despite showing signs of exhaustion, her beautiful features were made pleasant by a warm smile. "I'd been thinking much the same about you and, as I too doubted whether I could get away with cheating, I settled upon taking what you had brought with you and going on my merry way before the rest of your motley crew arrived." Touching her bruised cheek gingerly with a finger, she went on, "It never occurred to me that we might be birds of a feather."

"Or me," Belle seconded, removing the ruined blouse and, tossing it to the floor, indicating the knees that showed through her torn tights. "We could have saved losing some of our feathers if we'd told each other our real names in the first place. The one you're using ought to have warned me off. I know it sounds 'teddibly British, don't you know,' but *nobody* could really have a name like 'the Honorable Drusilla St. John-Belleweather.' "

"I'll have to tell the Honorable Drusilla that the next time we take tea together," the honey blonde commented. "She'll be rather miffed."

"I'd be more than *rather miffed* if I'd been saddled with a name like that," the lady outlaw stated. "Although some folks might say the same about mine. Disappointing as it must be, happen you've heard tell of me, I'm Belle Starr."

"I'd say you made me see stars, old thing, but you've probably heard something like it so *many* times before," the Englishwoman replied. "Yes, I do believe I *may* have heard of you. But if you think 'Drusilla St. John-Belleweather' sounds too British to be true, my full name is Amelia Penelope Diana Benkinsop. It's far too much of a mouthful, though, so my *friends* call me 'Benkers.' "

"Hi, *Benkers*," Belle greeted, and, rising from the easy chair as the honey blonde stood up, they walked forward to shake hands.

23

I'VE NEVER PULLED A JAILBREAK

"Gracious, Florence," Belle Starr exclaimed, needing only one glance to realize something of a very disturbing and serious nature must be responsible for the hurried arrival of her visitor. Rising from the dressing table at which she had been writing a letter, she went on, "Whatever's wrong?"

"It's Miss Benkers!" the newcomer replied in a voice that, although devoid of any discernible regional accent, established her origins as being British working class.

Five feet four inches in height, close to buxom, with tightly curled yellowish-red hair taken up in a neat pile on top of her head, Florence Drakefield was in her late twenties. Her normally cheerful attractive features were redolent of distress. Cut in a style calculated to enhance her curvaceous "hourglass" figure, the colorful dress she had on gave no indication that she was the maid who "Drusilla St. John-Belleweather" had implied was not deserving of trust. While this was the capacity in which she was employed, the lady outlaw was neither surprised nor puzzled by the obvious concern she was displaying.

"What's happened to her?" Belle demanded.

"S—she's been done to rights," Florence gasped, the heaving of her imposing bosom caused as much by deep emotion as the exertion of hurrying to deliver the news.

"Done to rights?" Belle repeated, the term being new to her.

"She's had her collar felt and not a chance to take stoppo!" the maid explained. Then, seeing no sign of comprehension, she realized the British criminal jargon she was using in her perturbation was not understood, and she continued, "She's been arrested."

"The hell you say!" the lady outlaw snapped. "When did it happen?"

"About half an hour ago!" the maid replied, looking close to tears. "I—I—!"

"Come and sit down, honey," Belle suggested, crossing to take the distressed redhead by the arm and leading her gently toward the bed. "Then take your time and tell me how it happened."

Four days had elapsed since the lady outlaw had learned the true identity of the beautiful honey-blond Englishwoman she had selected as, by her standards, deserving to be fleeced!

Not only had Belle heard of Amelia Penelope Diana "Benkers" Benkinsop, but European criminals she had met gave the Englishwoman credit for having acquired a fame on their side of the Atlantic Ocean that equaled her own. Nevertheless, the discovery had come as a surprise.[1] Usually news passed quickly through the criminal element. In fact, even though she had stayed east of the Mississippi River, word of

---

1. *Some further information regarding Amelia Penelope Diana "Benkers" Benkinsop is given in* Footnotes 13 *and* 13a, APPENDIX ONE. *J.T.E.*

the last visit paid by Benkers to the United States had reached the lady outlaw. On this occasion, there had not been so much as a rumor of her presence from the gathering places for outlaws in Kansas or on the way to Austin.

Now they had met, considering the events of the evening, Belle had been willing to agree that the comparison between the Englishwoman and herself was justified!

Furthermore, in spite of the means by which they had become acquainted, a warm friendship had developed between the two far-from-law-abiding beauties!

After shaking hands, Benkers had offered to help tidy up the sitting room of the mansion. Learning she was correct in her assumption of how Belle had obtained access to such a location, the obvious respectability of which was calculated to lessen suspicion, she had insisted upon sharing the cost of hiring it, pointing out they could recoup the money by working together, using the premises to lure genuine victims into a game of poker. The offer had been accepted without hesitation. In addition to having taken a liking to the Englishwoman and feeling sure the association would prove profitable, the lady outlaw had not been averse to having an opportunity to show her skill and see how well the honey blonde could manipulate cards for the purposes of cheating.

With the room returned to the condition in which they had found it, Belle and Benkers had done what they could to repair the ravages caused to their appearances during the fight. Washing and tidying their hair had made passable improvements in that direction, although nothing could be done about the bruise on the Englishwoman's cheek. Nor, while the discarded skirts had served to conceal the holes in tights and stockings, was there any way in which the ruined blouses could be made to pass unnoticed in public. However, the lady outlaw had claimed these would not prove an insurmountable obstacle. Explaining why this was, she and the honey blonde had retrieved their money and left the mansion.

Having intended to walk back to the hotel from which she and Benkers had come, Belle had not arranged for the cab to collect them and the return journey was made on foot. Selecting a route that avoided lighted areas where the discrepancies of their attire might have attracted unwanted attention, she had taken her companion to the boardinghouse owned by her aunt. While on the way, remarking she had the means to protect them against molestation if the need should arise, she had learned the honey blonde too was armed. Benkers had also disclosed that, since commencing her present visit to the United States, she had been taught by members of Ole Devil Hardin's floating outfit to draw and fire from a Western-style gunbelt and holster the Webley Royal Irish Constabulary revolver she was carrying in her reticule. Having explained how she had made their acquaintance,[2] she had confirmed Belle's supposition that it was she who had swindled Owen O'Brien in Dallas. Reaching the lady outlaw's room without incident, the loan of a blouse and makeup to cover the bruise had made it possible for the Englishwoman to return to the hotel without anything untoward being noticeable about her appearance.

Meeting in the suite occupied by Benkers the following morning, Belle had been introduced to Florence Drakefield and learned that, far from being untrustworthy, she was a loyal and devoted employee. This had been a contradiction of the conclusion drawn previously by the lady outlaw regarding their relationship. In keeping with the role she was playing,

---

2. *Told in* BENGUINAGE IS DEAD! *J.T.E.*

the honey blonde had treated her maid with harsh severity in public and, when not required for her duties, Florence was staying in more humble accommodation elsewhere.

Having discovered they had much in common, particularly in their outlook on life, the more Belle and Benkers had seen of each other, the stronger had grown the bond between them. They had also found their association lucrative.

Approached with the proposition, the butler had been amenable and the pair had held two more poker games at the mansion. On each occasion, such was their individual and combined expertise, the victims had gone away without suspecting the losses sustained had resulted from anything other than an unfortunate run of the cards. Concluding it would be inadvisable to use the premises again, but enjoying their happy and profitable partnership too much to want to bring it to an end so soon, they had elected to work a confidence trick upon a wealthy, less than scrupulous businessman who had come to their attention.

"Did some of the women we took in the poker games have it done?" Belle asked, feeling sure that Benkers would not have risked jeopardizing their latest proposition by indulging in a private criminal activity and falling afoul of the law as a result.

"No!" Florence denied vehemently, having sat on the bed and made a visible effort to regain some control of her emotions. Then her expressive face registered indignation and, starting to rise, she went on, "You needn't *worry*, even if they had, Miss Benkers would *never* split on where to find you!"

"I never for a moment thought she would," Belle drawled, her manner reassuring. "But I can't start figuring out how I can help her until I know what's happened."

"Sorry, Miss Starr," the maid apologized, sinking back onto the quilt with an air of being mollified. "It's just that—!"

"I know, honey," the lady outlaw said gently, as the explanation was brought to an inconclusive end. "Tell me everything you know."

"You wouldn't think there could be such lousy luck!" Florence commenced, her tone bitter. "A bloody Pink-Eye recognized her from the last time she was over here and knew she's still wanted for a job she pulled in New York. So he brought the marshal and had her arrested to be held until he can arrange for her to be taken back."

"There has to be more to it than that," Belle asserted. "From what I know of him, with the kind of reputation she's made for herself and the company she's been keeping, the marshal would want something a whole heap stronger than just a Pink-Eye's word before he'd chance taking in 'the Honorable Drusilla St. John-Bellweather.' "

"He's been given *more*!" the maid replied angrily. "When he searched the suite, he found some tom that'd been stolen from another room in one of her bags."

"*Tom?*" the lady outlaw queried.[3]

"Jewelry," Florence translated, agitation once again having caused her to employ the jargon of British criminals.

"Benkers never mentioned having taken any to me," Belle commented, despite feeling sure the stolen property would not have been found so easily if she had done so.

"She never took the bloody stuff!" the maid denied. "That bastard Pink-Eye must have got in while neither of us was there and planted it."

---

3. *"Tom": abbreviation of "tom foolery," Cockney rhyming slang for jewelry. J.T.E.*

"I've heard of such things being done," the lady outlaw admitted. "Although, by all accounts, Allan Pinkerton always *says* he doesn't countenance his Pink-Eyes doing things like that."[4]

"This one did!"

"I'm not saying you're wrong, honey. The trouble is, I can't see the marshal being willing to take your word, or mine, that he did it. There's one chance, though. Have you any idea when the jewelry was taken?"

"Around noon yesterday. Does that help?"

"Not a whole heap." Belle sighed. "The only way we could prove Benkers has an alibi would be to tell how we were with the butler, paying him off for letting us cheat those women at the mansion."

"Then she's done to rights!" Florence estimated with a groan. "The Pink-Eye said she's sure to get jailed when he's got her back to New York."

"How did you get away?" the lady outlaw inquired, then raised her right hand in placatory gesture as she saw her words had been misconstrued. "Now don't take what I said the wrong way, honey. I'm more than pleased you did. Tell me everything that happened. Start from the beginning and try not to leave anything out."

---

4. *In the interests of fair play, the information supplied by Andrew Mark "Big Andy" Counter establishes that the man in question was no longer employed by the Pinkerton National Detective Agency. Having been discharged for similar malpractices, he had retained their identification documents, but was working for himself. Having caught the man who stole the jewelry, he had seen how he might turn it to extra use by giving the town marshal a reason to hold the Englishwoman while arrangements could be made for her extradition from Texas to New York. Therefore, he had released the actual thief with orders to leave Austin immediately and say nothing of what passed between them. All this was learned by Belle Starr later. J.T.E.*

"I was down in the lobby. Miss Benkers had told me to go and listen to what those 'votes for women' crowd were saying about some big parade they're holding tonight."

"I know the one she meant. It's going to be around the Capitol Building, and they're thinking of stirring up trouble."

"It sounded that way. Well, I was on my way back when I saw the marshal and that Pink-Eye going up ahead of me. I knew about the tom being nicked, but didn't think anything about it until I saw them making Miss Benkers let them into our rooms. They hadn't seen me and I listened at the door, which's how I found out what was going on. Then, when I heard they were fetching her out, I took stoppo and come here. You don't mind me coming, do you, miss? Only, I couldn't think of anybody else to turn to."

"I'd have been annoyed if you hadn't come," Belle drawled, thinking how fortunate it was that the most important of Benkers's belongings had been transferred to the boardinghouse as a precaution against the need for them to leave Austin hurriedly.

"Can you do *anything*?" Florence pleaded, close to tears.

"I don't know," the lady outlaw confessed. "One thing's for sure. There's no *legal* way of getting her out."

"Then she's done for," the maid moaned.

"Not if I can help it!" Belle claimed, pensively and yet with a ring of grim determination in her voice. "I've never pulled a jailbreak, but I've always been told birds of a feather stick together and, as sure as sin's for sale in Cowtown, I'm going to give it a try."

24

ALL WE HAD TO DO WAS WAIT

"If anybody had told me that I would ever be *grateful* to those awful *women*-women, I'd have thought they were daffy," Amelia Penelope Diana "Benkers" Benkinsop declared, reminding herself to keep walking in a manner suitable to the masculine attire she was wearing. "But, after all the dear girls have done for me, I'm *almost* sorry I let you browbeat me into helping fleece some of them."

"You've got the easiest brow I've ever come across to beat," Belle Starr asserted. Having had more practice, she was experiencing less difficulty in ensuring her gait matched the garb she had on, despite it also being that of the opposite gender. "Why you was like' to chomp, whomp and stomp me when I said it wasn't cricket—don't you Lime-Juicers say—to take advantage of those poor li'l ole Yankee soft-shells."

For the rest of her life, the lady outlaw would always claim the rescue of her English friend was her finest achievement!

Having set her mind to the task of freeing Benkers,

Belle had displayed a planning skill many a military commander would have envied!

Despite Florence Drakefield having suggested there might be better opportunities while the beautiful prisoner was being taken to New York, the lady outlaw had concluded there were factors that favored taking action without delay. For one thing, a rescue bid was unlikely to be expected so soon after Benkers had been taken into custody. Another reason, even more important, had been an appreciation of the benefits that might accrue as a result of an event that was scheduled to take place that night. Taking the latter into account, she had checked upon the various clothing and disguises stored in a well-concealed hiding place below the boardinghouse owned by her aunt, and had selected the costumes that she believed most suited to her purpose. Having explained what she meant to do to the maid, they had made arrangements for a speedy departure from Austin if they should meet with the anticipated success.

Everything hinged upon one factor!

It was common knowledge that some of the advocates for women's suffrage did not intend merely to parade in a passive fashion around the Capitol Building, but were determined to draw attention to their cause by actions intended to bring about their arrest. Therefore, Belle had felt sure the town marshal would assemble as strong a force as possible in an attempt to keep the peace. Clad in the fashion she had selected, she and the maid had kept watch from near the jailhouse and satisfied themselves that her summation was correct, thereby increasing Florence's admiration for her. As the maid had remarked, probably on no other occasion at that hour would there have been only two deputies present in the office.

Confronted by what appeared to be a pair of nuns, neither peace officer had been suspicious when asked if religious solace could be given to the only prisoner held in the cells at the rear of the building. Nor, presented with a half-empty bottle of good-quality whiskey supposedly taken from "a poor sinner who knew not what he did" and asked to dispose of what was left, had they resisted the temptation to sample the contents. In doing so, they had saved themselves from being subdued by less peaceful and painless measures. Proving as effective as when used against David Icke and Benkers, the potion that Belle had added to the liquor rendered them unconscious speedily.

Dragging the deputies into the cell area, the rescuers had used the keys from the desk in the office to set the honey blonde free. The removal of their habits had revealed that, in addition to wearing other clothing to be used when taking their departure, they had brought suitable attire—including her Webley Royal Irish Constabulary revolver and gunbelt—to replace the garments she was wearing.

Clad and armed as a cowhand, with a loose-fitting jacket to help conceal her feminine contours—as Belle was—Benkers had found the key on the ring that unlocked the safe in the office. While Florence kept watch on the street, dressed after the fashion of a "lady of easy virtue," they had retrieved such of her property as had been put there by the marshal. She had declined the suggestion of the maid that, as she had already been accused of stealing it, she should also take the jewelry that the supposed Pinkerton operative had hidden in her room and that was being retained as evidence for holding her until extradition could be arranged. The lady outlaw had agreed with the decision, and it was subsequently proved to have been justified.

Leaving the building, their activities in the office having gone unnoticed due to the fact that people who might otherwise have been in the vicinity had gone to watch the parade by the suffragettes at the Capitol Building, the three young women had made their way to the boardinghouse. Their arrival having also gone unquestioned, they had stayed no longer that was required to leave the nuns' habits in the secret hiding place. Arrangements had been made for their departure from Austin, including the means of transport, and their belongings had been made ready during the afternoon. They had not changed the clothing they were wearing, gambling upon it helping to prevent them from being connected with the escaped prisoner and her female resuers should the alarm be raised sooner than anticipated. This had not happened, and they were approaching their destination.

Hearing the sounds of a disturbance some distance away, Benkers had made the reference to the people who had unwittingly helped to bring about her liberation.

"I haven't mentioned it before, old thing, but you do tend to overexaggerate somewhat on occasion," the honey blonde remarked. "By the by, I haven't thought to ask, but what have you in mind for us after we've left this charming city?"

"We'll start by heading south, as if we're figuring on crossing the Rio Grande into Mexico," Belle replied. "Then, once we're clear of Travis County, we'll make a swing around and lie low at a safe place I know until we've found out how much of a hunt there's being made for you. When we know that, we can decide upon the best way to get you out of the country."

"It's your home range, as I believe you colonials put it," the honey blonde assented. "So I'll leave myself in your hands and plead insanity when we get arrested."

"How soon will they be after us?" Florence asked, walking arm in arm with the other two as might be expected of the kind of people they were pretending to be.

"Going by the racket over to the Capitol, we ought to have a good head start before the marshal gets to know what we've done," the lady outlaw estimated. Then she waved her free hand in the direction of the small livery stable, owned by a retired outlaw who was another trusted acquaintance. "Here we are, so we'll soon be on our way."

"I hope your friend will be there," Benkers commented, seeing no sign of life although the inside of the main barn was illuminated. "I'd like to give him something for his help."

"I've already attended to that," Belle answered. "Going by what they were saying, Sam and his boys were figuring on walking over to the Capitol to watch what's going on. He gave me the key to the storeroom and promised they'd leave the horses and rig ready before they left."

Entering the building, the Englishwoman found it appeared to be as the lady outlaw had claimed. There was no sign of anybody else present, but the fine buckskin gelding that she had used while traveling through Texas was saddled and an equally good-quality horse stood harnessed to a buckboard. Seeing everything as she expected, she led the way toward the animals.

"Hole it there and keep your hands still!"

Hearing the words, spoken in a harsh Chicago accent, Belle and her companions did as was ordered. Turning her head, she saw three men in travel-stained city-style clothing holding revolvers and coming toward them from empty stalls in which they had been hiding. She recognized one as Joseph "Church" Steeples and, from the family resemblance, concluded the other two were his brothers, Albert "High" and Wilfred "Little." Aware that they were too far apart for her to take any action, she made no attempt to do so. Much to her relief, Benkers was showing an equal grasp of the situation and refraining from making any kind of movement.

"Just like I told you, boys!" Church Steeples announced. "With that big buckskin of her'n saddled up and a buggy hitched ready, she was figuring on pulling out. All we had to do was wait for her to show up."

"You told us," admitted Little Steeples, tallest and youngest of the brothers, sounding just a trifle grudging. "Only, you reckoned it'd be Parson Higgert and that hot-assed gal of his with her, and these two ain't either of them."

"That makes it all the better," High Steeples claimed, running a lascivious gaze over Belle, Benkers, and Florence in turn. "It'll be one apiece now and more fun all way 'round."

"All right, Starr!" Church growled, directing a scowl at the middle sibling. Possessing greater intelligence, he wanted to prevent the import of the ill-advised remark from being appreciated by the women, causing them to raise a commotion before they could be taken somewhere there would be no chance of their being heard. "Don't give us any fuss and you won't get hurt. We're taking you to the jailhouse."

"Like hell that's what you're aiming to do!" Belle denied, wanting to ensure her companions were alerted to the fate she felt certain awaited them all. "There's no *legal* bounty, or open warrant, on me anywhere. So you're after the money you've been told I'm toting and you don't need to keep me alive to collect the rest of whatever Armond Chauvelin's promised you. He just wants my hide nailing to the wall."

Watching the reaction of the brothers to her words, the lady outlaw knew she was correct in her assumptions. Nor had these been difficult to draw. It was unlikely that the Frenchman would have been sufficiently trusting to have given them enough money to go to all the trouble it must have taken to find her. Therefore, in addition to whatever advance payment he had made, he had offered them further inducement by convincing them she would be carrying a large sum with her.

Under different circumstances, Belle might have felt a certain admiration for the skill and enterprise shown by the brothers. Having succeeded in picking up her trail, they had had the forethought to obtain a description of the horse she was using. Locating it and finding it saddled, they had deduced that she was planning to leave Austin and had waited in concealment, after the departure of Sam and his hostlers, for her to put in an appearance. However, having succeeded in capturing her, they had no reason to keep her alive. Nor, she was certain, would they spare either of her companions. In fact, the only reason they had not opened fire immediately was that they didn't want to bring people to investigate the shooting.

"Keep your goddamned yapper shut, Starr!" Church commanded. "And all of you stick your hands out so's Brother High can fasten 'em!"

"You've got me," the lady outlaw pointed out, without doing as ordered. "These girls have no part in this, so leave them behind."

"And have them telling all your buddies about us?" High scoffed. "Like hell we're leaving them to do that!"

"So you're taking us too, are you?" Benkers inquired, sounding mild.

"You can bet your goddamned life we are," High confirmed, oblivious of the prohibitive glare directed at him by Church. "So get your hands stuck out like you was told."

"Very well," honey blonde assented, showing no concern.

While speaking, Benkers swung her gaze briefly to Florence and gave an almost imperceptible nod. Having done so, hoping her faith in the maid and Belle would be justified, she looked to the front and began to raise her hands.

"Here!" Florence yelped, starting to walk toward High. "You've got no call to take *me*, mister. I've never seen these two before tonight. I thought they was just a couple of them posh women who're in town and liked girls instead of blokes."

"Get the hell back th—!" the middle sibling snarled, reaching with the intention of pushing the maid away.

Grabbing the hand that was coming toward her, Florence raised it and buried her teeth into it. Taken completely unawares, High gave out a yell of mingled pain and anger that produced the effect she knew her employer was seeking. However, she hoped Belle would also be ready to make the most of any opportunity that arose. From what she saw while hanging on to the hand she was biting, she had achieved what she was trying to do.

Despite being startled by the commotion, if Church and Little had been dealing with men, they would not have succumbed to the instinctive reaction to look around. However, although they had noticed the gunbelts worn by Belle and Benkers, they had discounted these as being no more than part of the masculine attire used as a disguise.

The brothers were making a very serious mistake!

Having seen the signal passed between her companions, the lady outlaw was prepared for whatever might happen. As soon as the revolver that Church was pointing at her wavered from its alignment, she sent her right hand flashing downward. Grasping the butt of the Manhattan Navy Model revolver, she began to lift it. Thumbing back the hammer, as the six-and-a-half-inch barrel cleared the lip of the fast-draw holster, she fired at waist level and by instinctive alignment. Such was the skill she had acquired by much practice, she sent the .36-caliber bullet into the center of the bounty hunter's forehead and killed him instantly.

Possessing complete faith in Florence's ability to create the desired distraction, although not quite so fast as the lady outlaw, Benkers had been even more ready to respond when it came. In fact, she started reaching for her Webley Royal Irish Constabulary revolver an instant before Belle's draw was commenced. However, despite the advantage offered by the shorter barrel, the shot she got off came a fraction of a second later. The result was just as effective. Directing the lead in the way she knew it must go, aware that the man would show no mercy to herself and her friends, she shot to kill. Flying as was intended, the bullet took Little in the left breast and, tearing apart his heart, spun him in a lifeless twirl across the barn.

Satisfied she had played her part, Florence opened her mouth and flung herself away from High. On the point of turning his revolver upon her, he heard the shots fired by the other women. Seeing what had happened to his brothers, he changed his intentions. Starting to swing the weapon toward Belle and Benkers, finding himself the object of their attentions, he did not know which of them would pose the greater threat. Nor was he given a chance to make the decision. Aware of the danger, both responded to it instantly. Their revolvers spoke almost simultaneously, and either bullet would have proved fatal. Thrown backward, the last of the bounty hunters was dead before he joined the corpses of his brothers on the floor.

"*Gracias*, Benkers, Florence," the lady outlaw said quietly, a quick glance assuring her they had nothing further to fear from the three men. Lowering the smoking Manhattan and listening for anything to suggest the shooting was bringing people to investigate, she went on, "I'm sorry I got you into this!"

"You couldn't have guessed they'd be here," the honey blonde replied. "And, unless I've misjudged them completely, they meant to kill us as well as you."

"You hadn't misjudged them," Belle claimed, holstering the revolver and taking a key from the pocket of her jacket. "Here, Florence, start getting our gear out of the storeroom. Help me to calm down the horses, Benkers. There's nobody coming yet, but the sooner we're on our way, the better."

IN CONCLUSION

Not only was the escape from Austin effected without further incident, the plan proposed by Belle Starr proved equally successful.

Several factors allowed Amelia Penelope Diana "Benkers" Benkinsop and Florence Drakefield to leave the United States unhindered by being sought as fugitives.

Due to the disturbances at the Capitol Building having led to a number of arrests, by the time the town marshal of Austin learned of the escape, he had other problems demanding his attention. When he was at liberty to give his full attention to the matter, various aspects combined to lessen his urge to recapture the departed prisoner. The fortuitous arrival of two genuine operatives for the Pinkerton National Detective Agency exposed the man responsible for the arrest as a fake and he fled to avoid being subjected to their attentions. If the jewelry had been taken from the safe, its owner being of some importance, the marshal would have felt obliged to take steps to recover it. Under the circumstances, having no liking for "Pink-Eyes" and Yankees in general, he had felt disinclined to cause himself all the extra work he knew would ensue from arranging extradition should he be successful in the hunt for her. Despite concluding she had been involved, on learning the identity of the Steeples brothers and having an even greater aversion for bounty hunters, he had also guesses what had happened. Considering the trio had met the fate they deserved, he saw no reason to take action on their account. Therefore, the problems envisaged by the lady outlaw failed to materialize.

When satisfied it was safe to do so, Belle accompanied Benkers and Florence from Texas. They went their separate ways in Oklahoma Territory, after visiting her parents. Going to Kansas, where a friend was running a prosperous saloon in Mulrooney, the honey blonde had a further adventure before she and her maid arrived at New York and took passage on a boat to England.[1]

---

1. *Told in* Part Five, Belle "the Rebel Spy" Boyd in "The 'Butcher's' Fiery End," J.T.'S LADIES. *J.T.E.*

APPENDIX ONE

Throughout the years we have been writing, we have frequently received letters asking for various Western terms, or incidents to which we refer, to be explained in greater detail. While we do not have the slightest objection to receiving such mail, we have found it saves much time-consuming repetition to include those most often requested in each volume. We ask all our "old hands" who have read them before to bear with us and remember there are always "new chums" coming along who have not.

1. *Introduced in 1873, the Colt Model P "Single Action Army" revolver—with a caliber of .45 instead of the traditional .44—became popularly know as the "Peacemaker." Production continued until 1941, when it was taken out of the line to make way for the more modern firearms required in World War II. Over* three hundred and fifty thousand *were manufactured in practically every handgun caliber—with the exception of the .41*

and .44 *Magnums, which were not developed during the first production period—from .22 Rimfire to .476 Eley. However, the majority fired .45 or .44–40. The latter, given the name "Frontier Model," handled the same ammunition and powder charge of forty grains used in the Winchester Model of 1873 rifle and carbine.*

1a. *The barrel lengths of the production line Model P could be from three inches in the "Storekeeper" Model, which did not have an extractor rod, to sixteen inches in the "Buntline Special." The latter also was offered with an attachable metal "skeleton" butt stock, allowing it to be used as an extemporized carbine. However, the main barrel lengths were: Cavalry, seven and a half inches; Artillery, five and a half; Civilian, four and three-quarters.*

1b. *Popular demand, said to have been caused by the upsurge of action-escapism-adventure Western series on television, brought the Peacemaker back into the production line during 1955 and it is still being manufactured. For the first time, a model named the "Buntline Special"—albeit with a barrel only twelve inches long—allegedly due to the use of such a weapon by actor Hugh O'Brien while starring in the* WYATT EARP *television series, came into being.*

2. *We are frequently asked why it is the Belle Starr we describe is so much more shapely and attractive than portrayed in photographs that appear in various books. The researches of fictionist genealogist Philip José Farmer—author of, among numerous other works, the incomparable* TARZAN ALIVE, A Definitive Biography Of Lord Greystoke, *and* DOC SAVAGE, His Apocalyptic Life—*with whom we have consulted, have established that the "Belle Starr" to whom we refer*

*is not the same person as another equally famous
bearer of the name. However, the Counter
family have requested that we and Mr. Farmer
keep her true identity a secret, and we intend to
do so.*

3. *We strongly suspect that the trend in film and television Westerns made since the early 1960s to portray all cowhands as longhaired, heavily bearded,
and filthy stems less from the desire of the production companies to portray "realism" than because
there were so few actors—particularly to play sup-
porting roles—who were short-haired and clean-
shaven. Also because the "liberal" elements who
were gaining control of the mass entertainment
media seem to obtain some form of ego trip by
showing dirty habits, conditions, and appearances. In our extensive reference library, we
cannot find even a dozen photographs of actual
cowhands—as opposed to Army scouts, mountain
men, and old-time gold prospectors—with long
hair and bushy beards. In fact, our reading on the
subject and conversations with friends in the
modern West have led us to assume the term "long
hair" was one of opprobrium in the Old West and
Prohibition eras, just as it still is in cattle-raising
country today.*

4. *"Make wolf bait": one term meaning to kill. It
derived from the practice in the Old West, when a
range was infested by stock-destroying predators—
not necessarily just wolves, but mountain lion,
black or grizzly bears, and coyotes—of slaugh-
tering an animal and, having poisoned the car-
cass, leaving it where it fell to be devoured by the
carnivores.*

5. *"Gone To Texas": at odds with the law, generally
in the United States of America at the time the
saying came into general usage. Many wanted*

men and fugitives from justice entered Texas during the colonization period—which had commenced in the early 1820s, due to the Mexican government offering land to "Anglos" so they would act as a "buffer state" against marauding Comanche Indians—and continued until annexation as a State of the Union on February the 16th, 1846. Before the latter became a fact, such miscreants had known there was little danger of being arrested and extradited by the local authorities. Therefore, like Kenya from the 1920s until the outbreak of World War II, in spite of the great number of honest, law-abiding, and hard-working folks who genuinely wished to make their homes there, Texas during the days before independence was obtained from Mexican domination gained a reputation for being a "place in the sun for shady people."

6. *"Mason-Dixon" line, also erroneously called the "Mason-Dixie" line. The boundary between Pennsylvania and Maryland as surveyed in 1763–67 by the Englishmen Charles Mason and Jeremiah Dixon. It became known as the dividing line separating the Southern "Slave" and Northern "Free" States.*

7. *"New England": The northeast section of the United States, including Massachusetts, New Hampshire, Maine, Vermont, Connecticut, and Rhode Island, which was first settled primarily by people from the British Isles.*

8. *"Light a shuck": cowhands' expression for leaving hurriedly. It derives from the habit in night camps of trail drives and roundups on the open range of supplying "shucks"—dried corncobs—to be lit and used for illumination by anybody who had to leave the campfire and walk in the darkness. As the "shuck" burned away very quickly, a*

*person had to move fast if wanting to benefit from
its light.*

9. *In the Old West, the jurisdictional powers of
various types of law-enforcement agencies were
established as follows. A town marshal, sometimes
called "constable" in smaller places, and his
deputies were confined to the limits of the town or
city who appointed them. A Sheriff was elected by
and confined to his own county as were his
deputies. Texas and Arizona Rangers could go
anywhere within their respective States, but were
technically required to await an invitation by the
appropriate local peace officers before partici-
pating in an investigation. During the Prohibition era, as we explain in the* Alvin Dustine
"Cap" Fog *series, Company "Z" of the Texas
Rangers were allowed to initiate operations without awaiting an invitation. Although a United
States marshal had jurisdiction everywhere in the
country, his main function was the investigation of
"Federal" crimes.*

10. *The high heels and sharp toes of boots worn by
cowhands were functional rather than merely
decorative. The former enabled a foot to be slipped
into or out of a stirrup iron in an emergency. In
addition to helping hold the boot into the stirrup
iron more firmly, the latter could be spiked into
the ground as an aid to controlling an animal
that was roped when afoot.*

11. *"Summer name": an alias. A person in the Old
West could supply any name he or she wished on
being introduced. The only acceptable way in
which to express doubt was to ask, "Is that your
summer name?"*

12. *"Pick up his toes": to inflict punishment. The term
was derived from the name cowhands gave to a
roping throw intended to trap the forefeet of an*

animal while it was in motion. Generally, the method was employed only to punish a horse that persisted in breaking out of the wrangler's rope corral when part of a remuda. *While extremely dangerous to carry out, the throw was used on a basis of "kill or cure." If the offender was allowed to go unchecked, the other members of the* remuda *could pick up the habit. A description of how the throw was made and its effect is given in* TRAIL BOSS.

13. *Other incidents that took place during the visit of Amelia Penelope Diana "Benkers" Benkinsop to the United States of America are recorded in* BEGUINAGE IS DEAD! *and* Part Five, Belle "the Rebel Spy" Boyd, "The Butcher's Fiery End." J.T.'S LADIES.

13a. *According to the researches of Philip José Farmer,* q.v., *by tradition, regardless of who the father might be, the eldest daughter always bore the name "Amelia Penelope Diana Benkinsop." Information regarding a descendant of "Benkers" can be found in* BLONDE GENIUS *and* Part Two, Amanda "the School Swot" Tweedle, "Fifteen The Hard Way," J.T.'S LADIES.

APPENDIX TWO

Raven Head, only daughter of Chief Long Walker, war leader of the *Pehnane*—Wasp, Quick Stinger, or Raider—Comanches' Dog Soldier lodge and his French-Creole *pairaivo*,[1] married an Irish Kentuckian adventurer, Sam Ysabel, but died giving birth to their first child. Baptized "Loncey Dalton Ysabel"— although we doubt whether any minister of a church officiated—the boy was raised after the fashion of the *Nemenuh*.[2] With his father away on the family business of mustanging—catching and breaking wild horses[3]—and smuggling, his education had largely been left in the hands of his maternal grandfather.[4] From Chief Long Walker, he had learned all those things a Comanche warrior must know: How to ride the wildest freshly caught mustang, or make a trained animal subservient to his will when raiding, a polite name for the favorite pastime of the male *Nemenuh*, stealing horses. To follow the faintest tracks and just as effectively conceal signs of his own passing.[5] To locate hidden enemies, or keep out of sight himself when the need arose. To move in silence through the thickest cover and on the darkest nights. To know the ways of wild creatures and, in some cases, imitate their calls so that even others of their kind might be fooled.[6]

The boy had proved an excellent pupil in all the subjects. Furthermore, he had inherited his father's Kentuckian rifle-shooting prowess and, while not *real* fast on the draw—taking slightly over a second to bring out and fire his weapon, whereas a top hand could practically halve that time—he performed passably with his Colt Second Model Dragoon revolver. By his exceptional skill in wielding one, he had won his Comanche man-name, *Cuchilo,* the Spanish word for "Knife." It was claimed by those best qualified to know that he could equal the alleged designer in performing with the massive and special type of blade that bore Colonel James Bowie's name.[7]

Joining his father in smuggling expeditions along the Rio Grande, the boy had become known to the Mexicans of the border country as *"Cabrito"*: a name that, although meaning a young goat, had arisen out of hearing white men refer to him as the Ysabel Kid and was spoken *very* respectfully in that context. Smuggling did not tend to attract those of a mild-mannered and pacific nature, but even the roughest and toughest of the bloody border's brood had soon come to acknowledge it did not pay to rile up Sam Ysabel's son. Little in the Kid's education and upbringing had been calculated to develop any over-inflated sense of the sanctity of human life. When crossed, he dealt with the situation in the manner of a *Pehnane* Dog Soldier—to which war lodge of most savage and efficient warriors he had earned initiation—swiftly and in an effectively deadly fashion.

During the War Between the States, the Kid and his father had commenced by riding as scouts for Colonel

John Singleton "the Grey Ghost" Mosby. Later, their specialized knowledge and talents had been converted to having them collect and deliver to the Confederate States authorities in Texas supplies that were run through the blockade imposed by the United States Navy into Matamoros, or that were purchased in other parts of Mexico. It had proved hard and dangerous work, but never more so than when they had become involved in the affairs of Belle "the Rebel Spy" Boyd.[8]

Soon after the end of the War, Sam Ysabel was murdered. While hunting for the killers, the Kid had met Captain Dustine Edward Marsden "Dusty" Fog and Mark Counter.[9] When the assignment upon which they were engaged was brought to its successful conclusion,[10] learning that the Kid no longer wished to continue the family business either as a mustanger or a smuggler, Dusty had offered him employment at the OD Connected ranch. It had been in the capacity of scout rather than cowhand that he had entered the service of the owner, General Jackson Baines "Ole Devil" Hardin, C.S.A.,[11] and his talents were frequently of the greatest use as a member of the floating outfit.[12]

The Kid's acceptance had been of the greatest benefit all around. The ranch obtained the services of an extremely loyal, capable, and efficient fighting man. Dusty acquired another trustworthy friend ready to stick by him through any kind of danger. For his part, the Kid was turned from a life of petty crime— with the ever-present possibility of his activities developing to serious lawbreaking—and became a most useful member of society. Peace officers and honest citizens might have found cause to feel grateful when he became law-abiding. His *Nemenuh* education would have made him a terrible and dangerous outlaw had he been driven to adopt a life of crime.

Obtaining his first repeating rifle—a Winchester Model of 1866, nicknamed the "Old Yellowboy" because of its brass frame, although it was first marketed as the "New, Improved Henry"—while in Mexico with Dusty and Mark, the Kid had soon become a master in its use. At the first Cochise County Fair in Arizona, despite having been compelled to use one of the newer model after his own was damaged in a fight, he had won first prize in the rifle-shooting competition against very stiff opposition. This was one of the legendary Winchester Model of 1873s that had qualified to be given the title "One of a Thousand."[13]

It was, in part, through the efforts of the Kid that the majority of the Comanche bands had agreed to go on to the reservation following the circumvented attempts to ruin the treaty-signing ceremony at Fort Sorrel.[14] Nor could Dusty have cleaned out the outlaw town called Hell without his assistance.[15] Although attempt to acquire the legendary weapon of Colonel Bowie had failed,[16] he had received a pocketknife made from the same superlative steel.[17] A chance meeting with Martha "Calamity Jane" Canary had resulted in his accompanying her when she went to claim a ranch she had inherited.[18]

1. Pairaivo: *first, or favorite, wife. As in the case of other Comanche names, this is a phonetic spelling.*
2. Nemenuh: *"the People," the Comanches name for their nation. Frequently with good cause, present-day ethnic apologists notwithstanding, members of other Indian races called them* Tshaoh, *the Enemy People.*
3. *A description of some methods employed by mustangers is given in* .44 CALIBRE MAN *and* A HORSE CALLED MOGOLLON.

4. *Told in* COMANCHE.

5. *An example of the Ysabel Kid's ability to conceal his tracks is given in* Part One, "The Half Breed," THE HALF BREED.

6. *An example of how the Ysabel Kid turned his knowledge of wild animals and mimicry to good use is given in* Part Three, "A Wolf's a Knowing Critter," J.T.'S HUNDREDTH.

7. *Some researchers claim that the actual designer of the knife was the eldest brother of James Bowie, Rezin Pleasant, and it was made by the master cutler, James Black, of Arkansas. Other authorities assert that it was manufactured by Jesse Cliffe, a white blacksmith employed on the Bowie family's plantation in Rapides Parish, Louisiana.*

7a. *As all James Black's bowie knives were handmade, there were slight variations in their dimensions. The specimen owned by the Ysabel Kid had a blade eleven and a half inches long, two and a half inches wide, and a quarter of an inch thick at the guard. According to W.D. "Bo" Randall of Randall-Made Knives, Orlando, Florida—a master cutler and authority on the subject— Bowie's knife weighed forty-three ounces, having a blade eleven inches long, two and a quarter inches wide, and three-eighths of an inch thick. His Model 12 "Smithsonian" bowie knife is modeled upon it. One thing all "bowie" type knives have in common is a "clip" point, where the last few inches of the otherwise unsharpened "back" of the blade joins and becomes an extension of the cutting edge in a concave arc, whereas a "spear" point is formed by the two sides coming together in symmetrical curves.*

7b. *What happened to James Bowie's knife after his death in the final assault of the besieged Alamo*

Mission, *San Antonio de Bexar, Texas, on March the 6th, 1836, is told in* GET URREA *and* THE QUEST FOR BOWIE'S BLADE.

8. *Told in* THE BLOODY BORDER *and* BACK TO THE BLOODY BORDER (*U.S.A. Berkley 1978 edition retitled* RENEGADE). *Other appearances by Belle "the Rebel Spy" Boyd are made in* THE COLT AND THE SABRE, THE REBEL SPY, THE HOODED RIDERS, THE BAD BUNCH, SET A-FOOT, TO ARMS! TO ARMS! IN DIXIE!, THE SOUTH WILL RISE AGAIN, Part Eight, "Affair of Honour," J.T.'S HUNDREDTH, THE REMITTANCE KID, THE WHIP AND THE WAR LANCE *and* Part Five, "The Butcher's Fiery End," J.T.'S LADIES.

9. *Details of the careers and special qualifications of Captain Dustine Edward Marsden "Dusty" Fog, C.S.A., and Mark Counter are given in various volumes of the* Civil War *and* Floating Outfit *series.*

10. *Told in* THE YSABEL KID. *Our original title for this volume was* DUSTY FOG, *but the substitution was made without consultation or explanation by our first publishers.*

11. *Details of the career of General Jackson Baines "Ole Devil" Hardin are given in the* Ole Devil Hardin *series,* Part Four, "Mr. Colt's Revolving Cylinder Pistol," J.T.'S HUNDREDTH—*which cover his early life—and the* Civil War *and* Floating Outfit *series. How he was crippled in a riding accident is described in* Part Three, "The Paint," THE FASTEST GUN IN TEXAS *and his death is reported in* DOC LEROY, M.D.

12. *"Floating outfit": a group of from four to six cowhands employed by a large ranch to work the more distant sections of its range. Taking food in*

a chuck wagon, or "greasy sack" on the back of a pack animal, they would be away from the ranch house for several days at a time. For that reason, they were selected from the best and most trustworthy members of the crew. Because of the prominence of General Hardin in the affairs of Texas, the OD Connected ranch's floating outfit were frequently sent to assist such of his friends who were in difficulty or endangered.

13. *When manufacturing the extremely popular Winchester Model of 1873, the makers selected those having barrels found to shoot with exceptional accuracy to be fitted with set triggers and given a special fine finish. Originally, these were inscribed, "1 of 1,000," but this was later changed to script, "One of a Thousand." However, the title was a considerable understatement. Only one hundred and thirty-six out of a total production of 720,610 rifles qualified for the distinction. Those of a grade lower in quality were given the name "One of a Hundred," but only seven were so designated. The practice commenced in 1875 and was discontinued in 1878, allegedly because the management decided it was not a good sales policy to suggest the company was producing different grades of the gun.*

14. *Told in* SIDEWINDER.

15. *Told in* HELL IN THE PALO DURO *and* GO BACK TO HELL.

16. *Told in* THE QUEST FOR BOWIE'S BLADE.

17. *One occasion when the life of the Kid was saved by the pocketknife is described in* OLD MOCCASINS ON THE TRAIL.

18. *Told in* WHITE STALLION, RED MARE.